6

STONE ARCH BOOKS
a capstone imprint

STONE ARCH BOOKS™

Published in 2013
A Capstone Imprint
1710 Roe Crest Drive
North Mankato, MN 56003
www.capstonepub.com

Originally published by DC Comics in the U.S. in single magazine form as Young Justice #6.

DC Comics
1700 Broadway, New York, NY 10019
A Warner Bros. Entertainment Company

Printed in China by Nordica.
0413/CA21300442
032013 007226NORDF13

Cataloging-in-Publication Data is available at the Library of Congress website:
ISBN: 978-1-4342-6038-3 (library binding)

Summary: Campfire bonding continues as the members of the team share their background stories as well as their hopes and fears. But when do these team-building exchanges cross over into TMI territory? How about when Superboy tells everyone how he's thinking of taking out Superman?!

STONE ARCH BOOKS

Ashley C. Andersen Zantop *Publisher*
Michael Dahl *Editorial Director*
Donald Lemke & Sean Tulien *Editors*
Heather Kindseth *Creative Director*
Brann Garvey & Alison Thiele *Designers*
Kathy McColley *Production Specialist*

DC COMICS

Scott Peterson & Jim Chadwick *Original U.S. Editors*
Michael McCalister *U.S. Assistant Editor*
Mike Norton *Cover Artist*

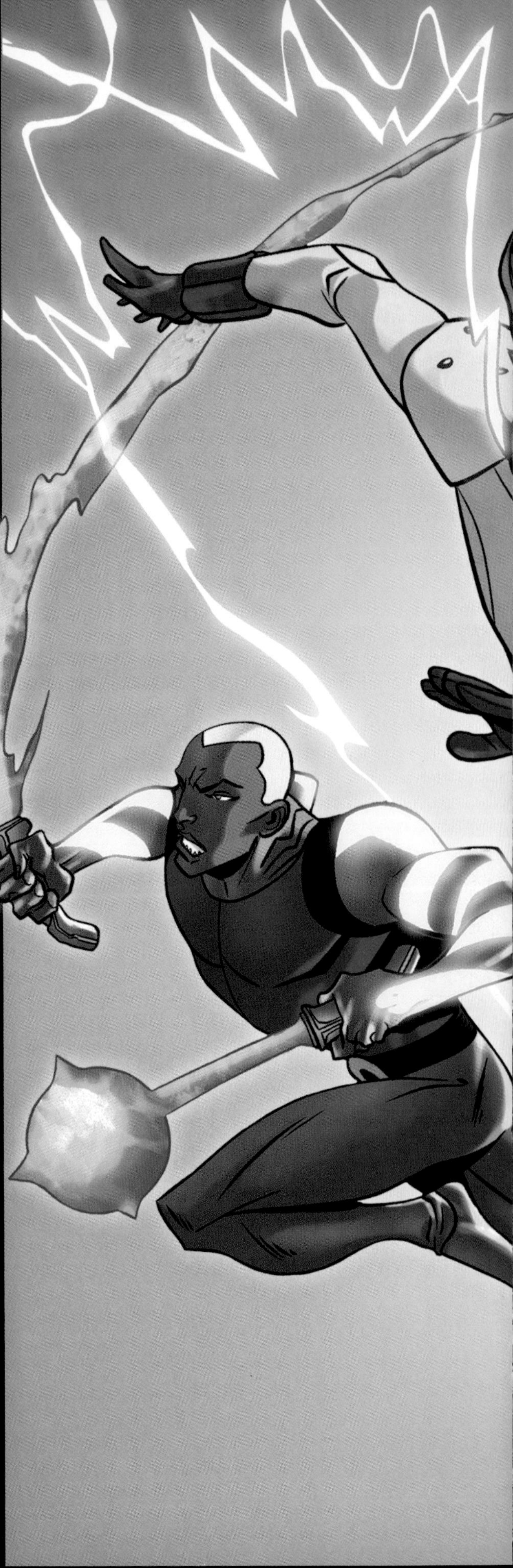

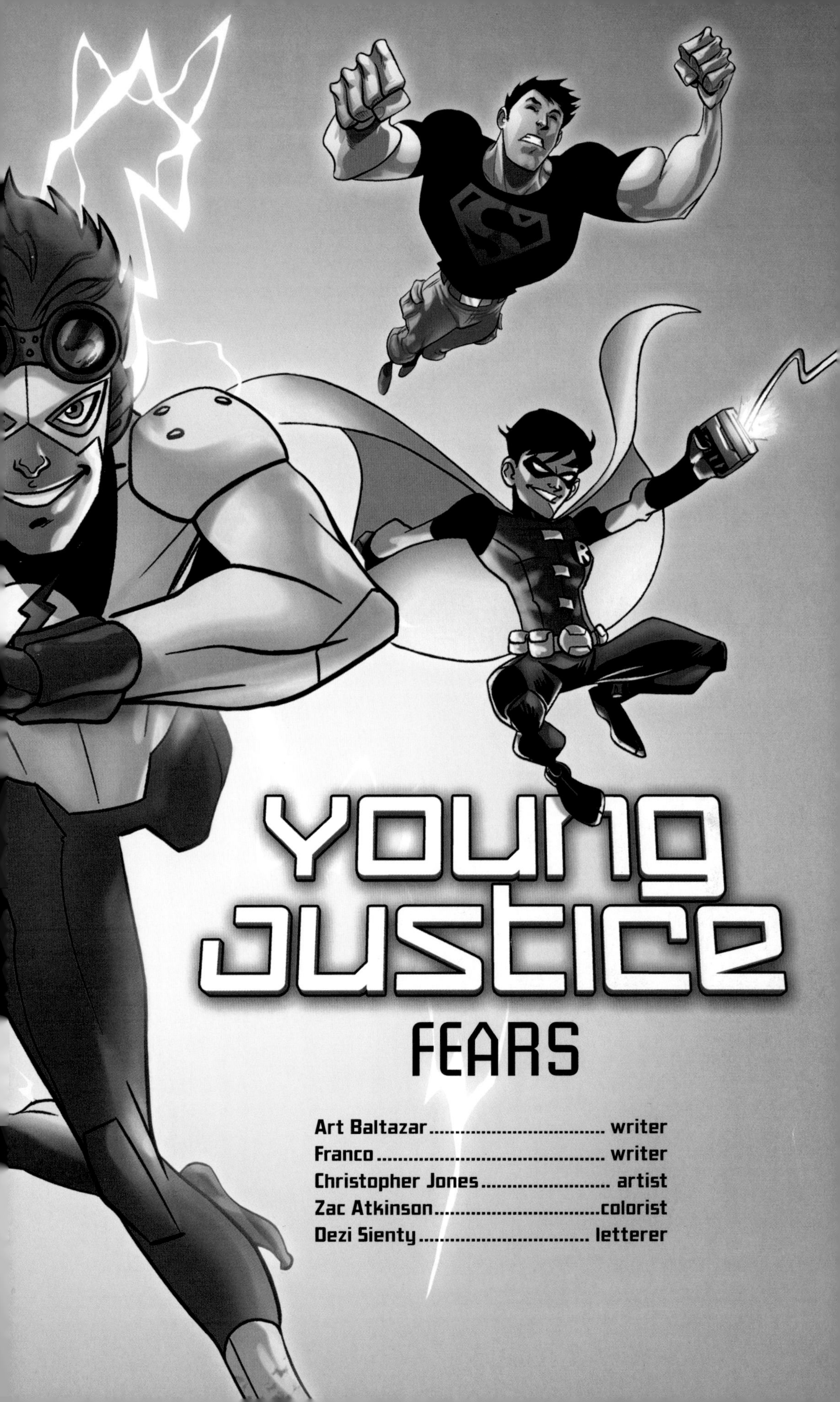

YOUNG JUSTICE

FEARS

Art Baltazar.................................... writer
Franco.. writer
Christopher Jones......................... artist
Zac Atkinson.................................colorist
Dezi Sienty.................................. letterer

young Justice™

AQUALAD

AGE: 16   SECRET IDENTITY: Kaldur' Ahm

BIO: Aquaman's apprentice; a cool, calm warrior and leader; totally amphibious with the ability to bend and shape water.

SUPERBOY

AGE: 16   SECRET IDENTITY: Conner Kent

BIO: Cloned from Superman; a shy and uncertain teenager; gifted with super-strength, infrared vision, and leaping abilities.

ARTEMIS

AGE: 15   SECRET IDENTITY: Classified

BIO: Green Arrow's niece; a dedicated and tough fighter; extremely talented in both archery and martial arts.

KID FLASH

AGE: 15   SECRET IDENTITY: Wally West

BIO: Partner of the Flash; a competitive team member, often lacking self-control; gifted with super-speed.

ROBIN

AGE: 13   SECRET IDENTITY: Dick Grayson

BIO: Partner of Batman; the youngest member of the team; talented acrobat, martial artist, and hacker.

MISS MARTIAN

AGE: 16   SECRET IDENTITY: M'gann M'orzz

BIO: Martian Manhunter's niece; polite and sweet; ability to shape-shift, read minds, transform, and fly.

THE STORY SO FAR...

After sharing origin stories around a campfire, Superboy revealed that he constantly thinks of destroying Superman, and Robin broods over the fact that he can't share his origin story with the others.

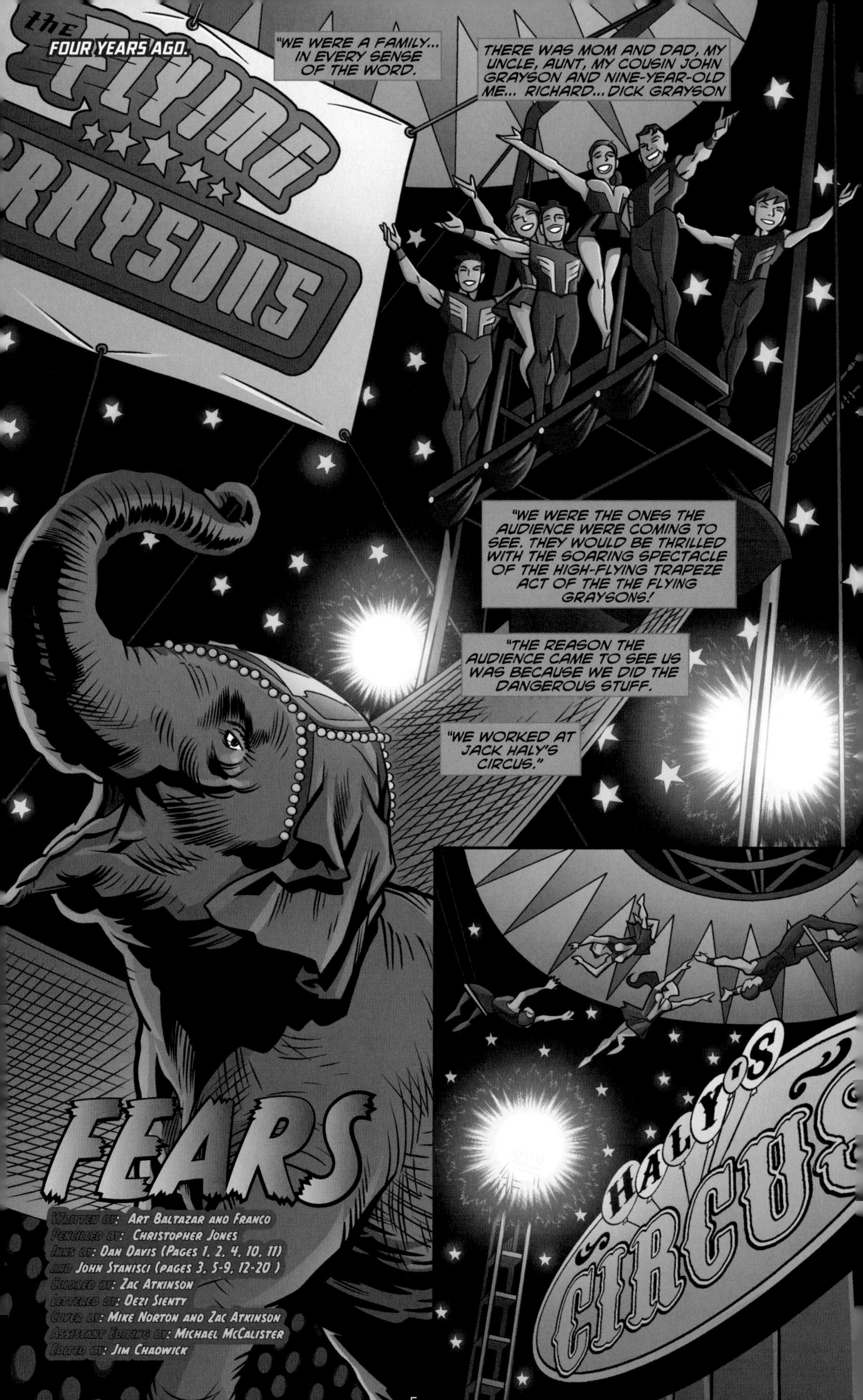
the FLYING GRAYSONS
FOUR YEARS AGO.
"WE WERE A FAMILY... IN EVERY SENSE OF THE WORD.
THERE WAS MOM AND DAD, MY UNCLE, AUNT, MY COUSIN JOHN GRAYSON AND NINE-YEAR-OLD ME... RICHARD... DICK GRAYSON
"WE WERE THE ONES THE AUDIENCE WERE COMING TO SEE. THEY WOULD BE THRILLED WITH THE SOARING SPECTACLE OF THE HIGH-FLYING TRAPEZE ACT OF THE THE FLYING GRAYSONS!
"THE REASON THE AUDIENCE CAME TO SEE US WAS BECAUSE WE DID THE DANGEROUS STUFF.
"WE WORKED AT JACK HALY'S CIRCUS."
FEARS
Written by: Art Baltazar and Franco
Pencilled by: Christopher Jones
Inks by: Dan Davis (Pages 1, 2, 4, 10, 11)
and John Stanisci (pages 3, 5-9, 12-20)
Colored by: Zac Atkinson
Lettered by: Dezi Sienty
Cover by: Mike Norton and Zac Atkinson
Assistant Editing by: Michael McCalister
Edited by: Jim Chadwick
HALY'S CIRCUS

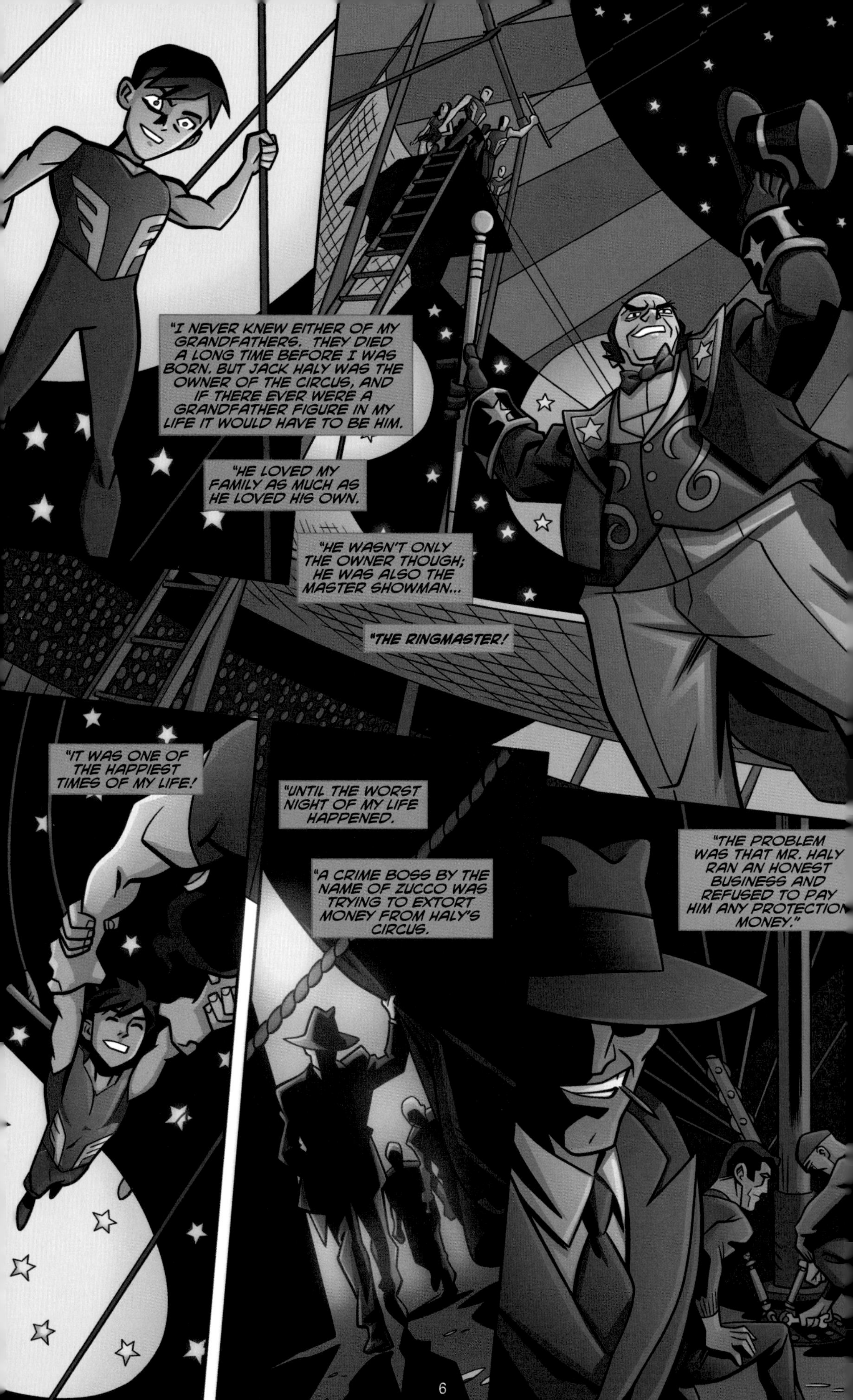
"I NEVER KNEW EITHER OF MY GRANDFATHERS. THEY DIED A LONG TIME BEFORE I WAS BORN. BUT JACK HALY WAS THE OWNER OF THE CIRCUS, AND IF THERE EVER WERE A GRANDFATHER FIGURE IN MY LIFE IT WOULD HAVE TO BE HIM.
"HE LOVED MY FAMILY AS MUCH AS HE LOVED HIS OWN.
"HE WASN'T ONLY THE OWNER THOUGH; HE WAS ALSO THE MASTER SHOWMAN...
"THE RINGMASTER!
"IT WAS ONE OF THE HAPPIEST TIMES OF MY LIFE!
"UNTIL THE WORST NIGHT OF MY LIFE HAPPENED.
"A CRIME BOSS BY THE NAME OF ZUCCO WAS TRYING TO EXTORT MONEY FROM HALY'S CIRCUS.
"THE PROBLEM WAS THAT MR. HALY RAN AN HONEST BUSINESS AND REFUSED TO PAY HIM ANY PROTECTION MONEY."

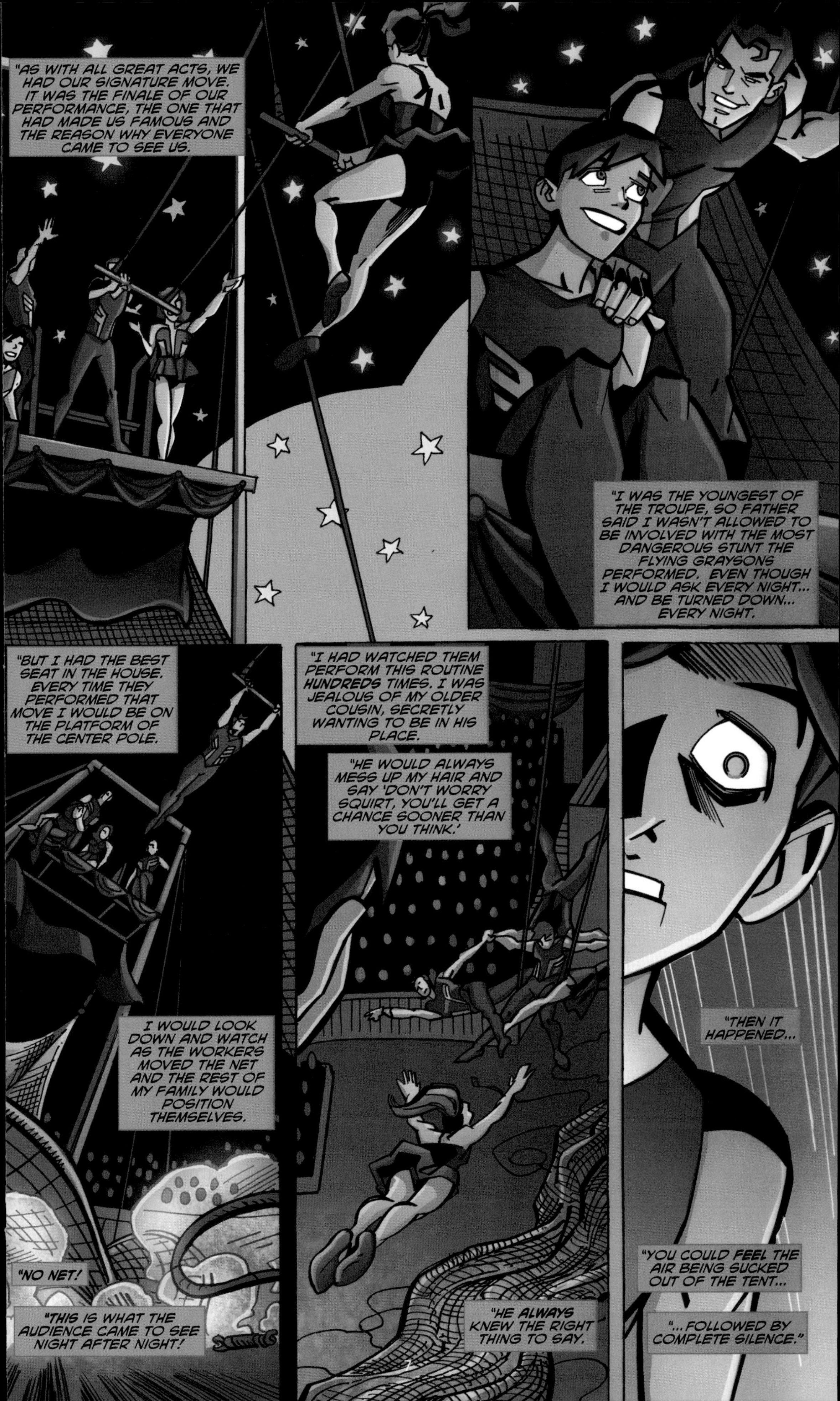
"AS WITH ALL GREAT ACTS, WE HAD OUR SIGNATURE MOVE. IT WAS THE FINALE OF OUR PERFORMANCE, THE ONE THAT HAD MADE US FAMOUS AND THE REASON WHY EVERYONE CAME TO SEE US.
"I WAS THE YOUNGEST OF THE TROUPE, SO FATHER SAID I WASN'T ALLOWED TO BE INVOLVED WITH THE MOST DANGEROUS STUNT THE FLYING GRAYSONS PERFORMED. EVEN THOUGH I WOULD ASK EVERY NIGHT... AND BE TURNED DOWN... EVERY NIGHT.
"BUT I HAD THE BEST SEAT IN THE HOUSE. EVERY TIME THEY PERFORMED THAT MOVE I WOULD BE ON THE PLATFORM OF THE CENTER POLE.
I WOULD LOOK DOWN AND WATCH AS THE WORKERS MOVED THE NET AND THE REST OF MY FAMILY WOULD POSITION THEMSELVES.
"NO NET!
"THIS IS WHAT THE AUDIENCE CAME TO SEE NIGHT AFTER NIGHT!
"I HAD WATCHED THEM PERFORM THIS ROUTINE HUNDREDS TIMES. I WAS JEALOUS OF MY OLDER COUSIN, SECRETLY WANTING TO BE IN HIS PLACE.
"HE WOULD ALWAYS MESS UP MY HAIR AND SAY 'DON'T WORRY SQUIRT, YOU'LL GET A CHANCE SOONER THAN YOU THINK.'
"HE ALWAYS KNEW THE RIGHT THING TO SAY.
"THEN IT HAPPENED...
"YOU COULD FEEL THE AIR BEING SUCKED OUT OF THE TENT...
"...FOLLOWED BY COMPLETE SILENCE."

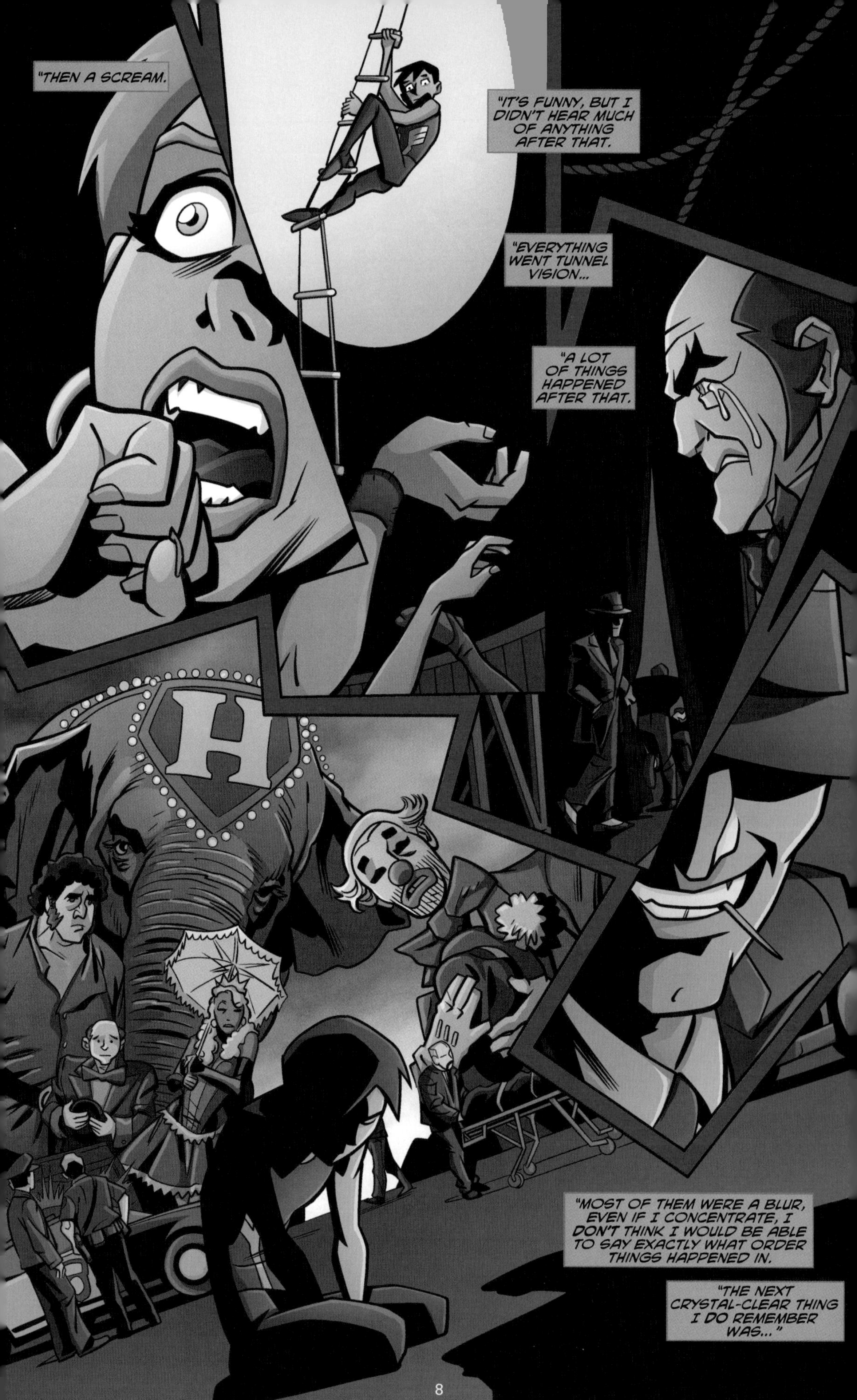
"THEN A SCREAM.
"IT'S FUNNY, BUT I DIDN'T HEAR MUCH OF ANYTHING AFTER THAT.
"EVERYTHING WENT TUNNEL VISION...
"A LOT OF THINGS HAPPENED AFTER THAT.
"MOST OF THEM WERE A BLUR, EVEN IF I CONCENTRATE, I DON'T THINK I WOULD BE ABLE TO SAY EXACTLY WHAT ORDER THINGS HAPPENED IN.
"THE NEXT CRYSTAL-CLEAR THING I DO REMEMBER WAS..."

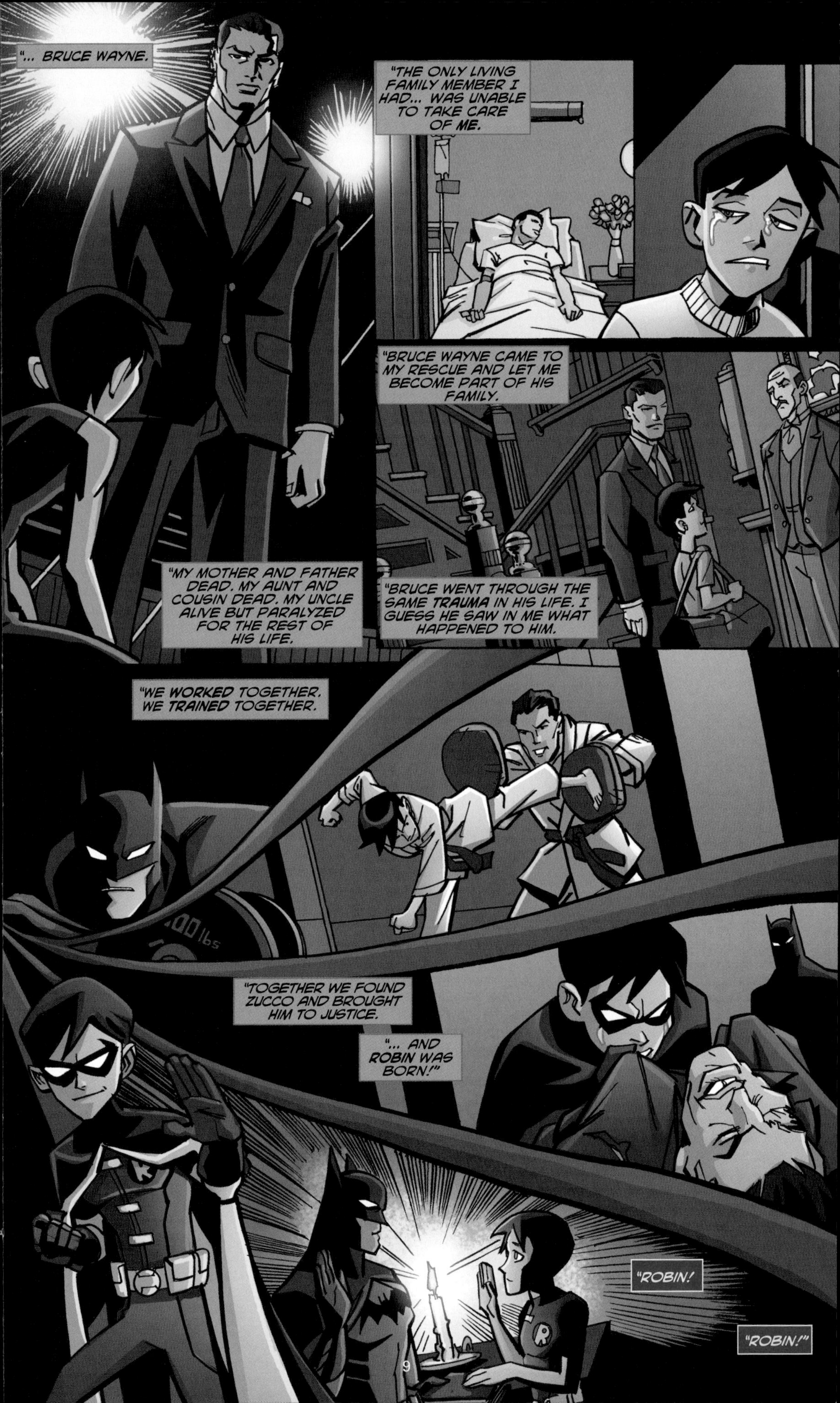
"... BRUCE WAYNE.
"THE ONLY LIVING FAMILY MEMBER I HAD... WAS UNABLE TO TAKE CARE OF ME.
"MY MOTHER AND FATHER DEAD. MY AUNT AND COUSIN DEAD. MY UNCLE ALIVE BUT PARALYZED FOR THE REST OF HIS LIFE.
"BRUCE WAYNE CAME TO MY RESCUE AND LET ME BECOME PART OF HIS FAMILY.
"BRUCE WENT THROUGH THE SAME TRAUMA IN HIS LIFE. I GUESS HE SAW IN ME WHAT HAPPENED TO HIM.
"WE WORKED TOGETHER. WE TRAINED TOGETHER.
"TOGETHER WE FOUND ZUCCO AND BROUGHT HIM TO JUSTICE.
"... AND ROBIN WAS BORN!"
"ROBIN!
"ROBIN!"

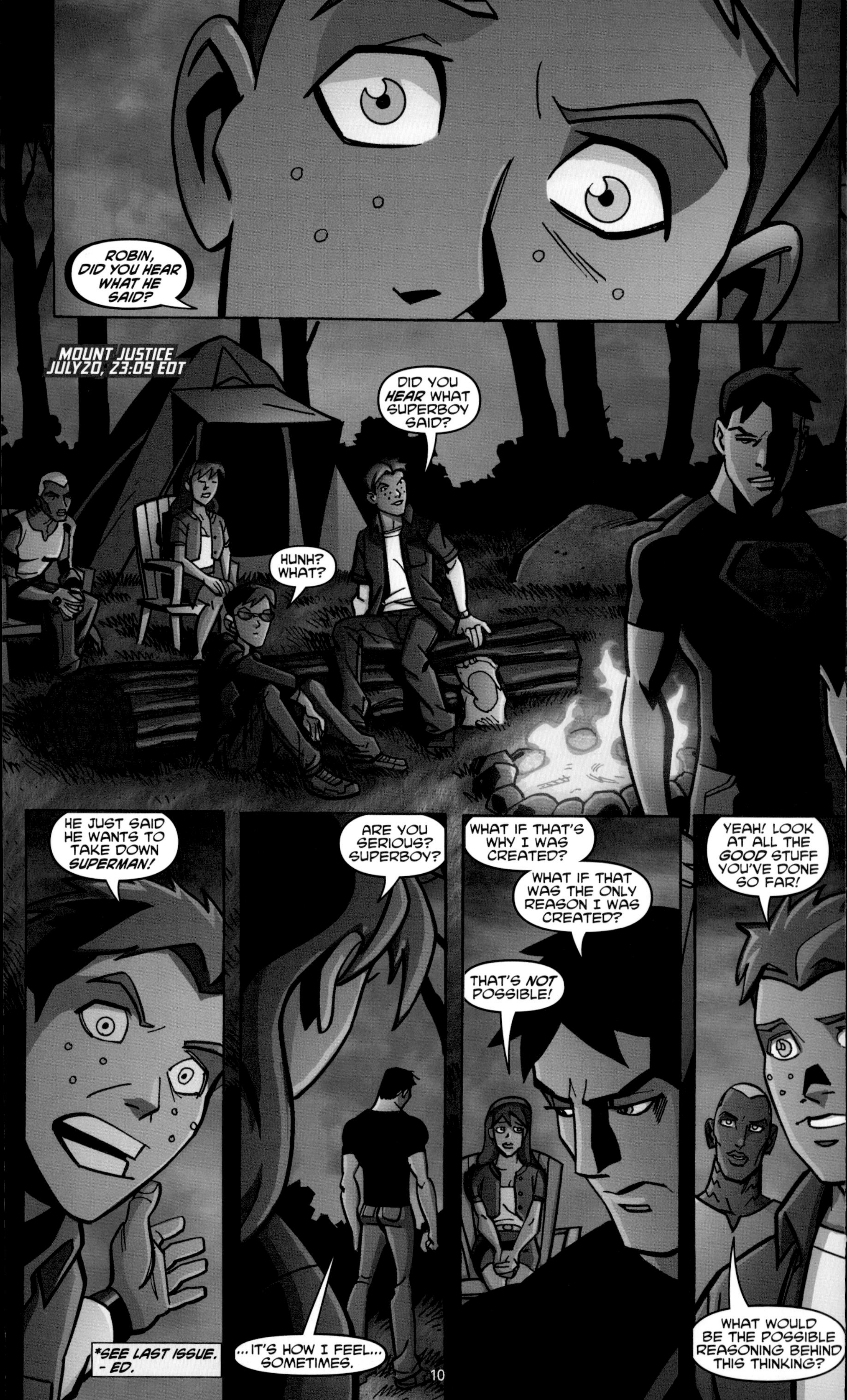

ROBIN, DID YOU HEAR WHAT HE SAID?
MOUNT JUSTICE
JULY20, 23:09 EDT
DID YOU HEAR WHAT SUPERBOY SAID?
HUNH? WHAT?
HE JUST SAID HE WANTS TO TAKE DOWN SUPERMAN!
ARE YOU SERIOUS? SUPERBOY?
...IT'S HOW I FEEL... SOMETIMES.
WHAT IF THAT'S WHY I WAS CREATED?
WHAT IF THAT WAS THE ONLY REASON I WAS CREATED?
THAT'S NOT POSSIBLE!
YEAH! LOOK AT ALL THE GOOD STUFF YOU'VE DONE SO FAR!
WHAT WOULD BE THE POSSIBLE REASONING BEHIND THIS THINKING?
*SEE LAST ISSUE. - ED.

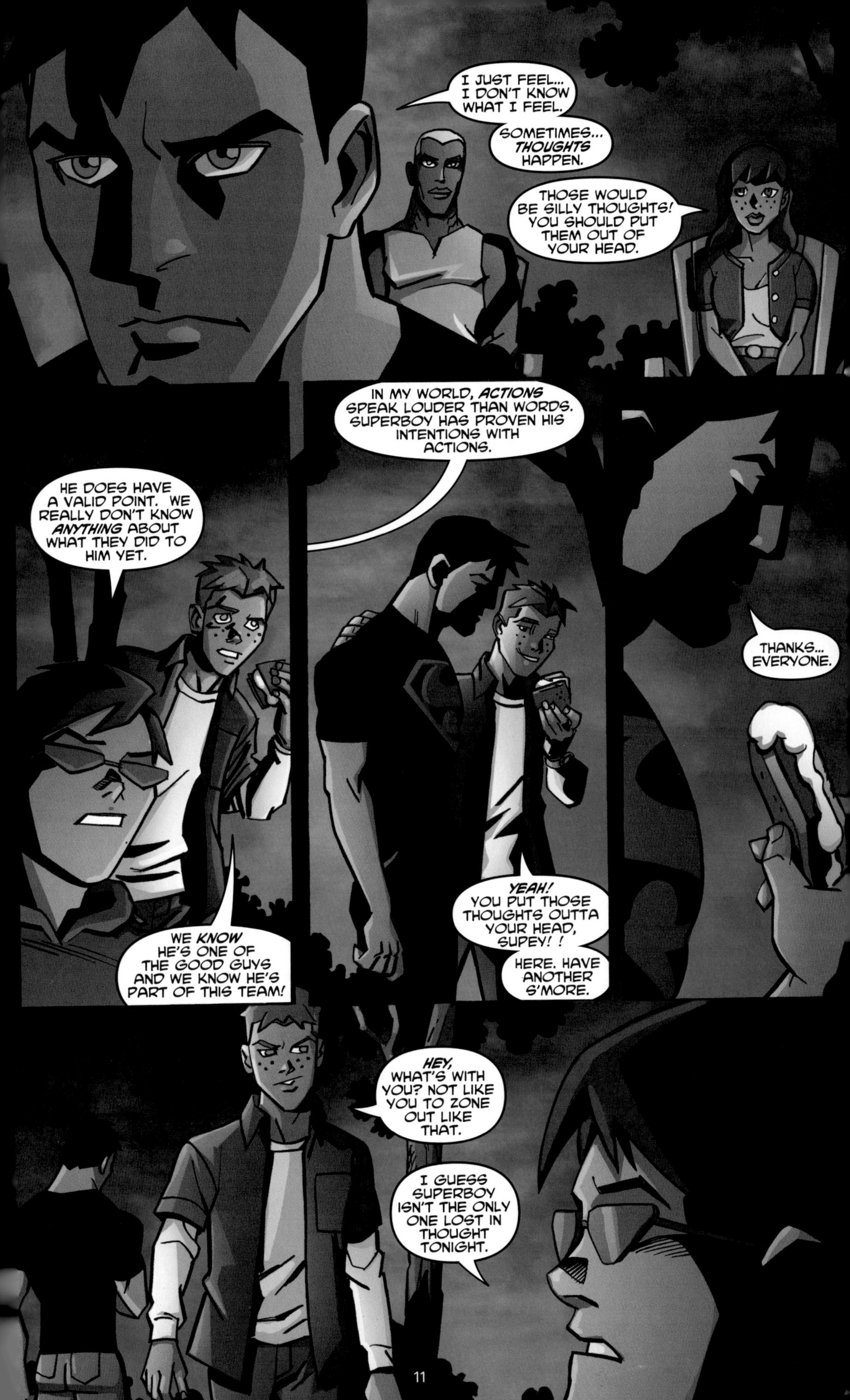
I JUST FEEL... I DON'T KNOW WHAT I FEEL.
SOMETIMES... *THOUGHTS* HAPPEN.
THOSE WOULD BE SILLY THOUGHTS! YOU SHOULD PUT THEM OUT OF YOUR HEAD.
HE DOES HAVE A VALID POINT. WE REALLY DON'T KNOW *ANYTHING* ABOUT WHAT THEY DID TO HIM YET.
WE *KNOW* HE'S ONE OF THE GOOD GUYS AND WE KNOW HE'S PART OF THIS TEAM!
IN MY WORLD, *ACTIONS* SPEAK LOUDER THAN WORDS. SUPERBOY HAS PROVEN HIS INTENTIONS WITH ACTIONS.
YEAH! YOU PUT THOSE THOUGHTS OUTTA YOUR HEAD, SUPEY! !
HERE. HAVE ANOTHER S'MORE.
THANKS... EVERYONE.
HEY, WHAT'S WITH YOU? NOT LIKE YOU TO ZONE OUT LIKE THAT.
I GUESS SUPERBOY ISN'T THE ONLY ONE LOST IN THOUGHT TONIGHT.

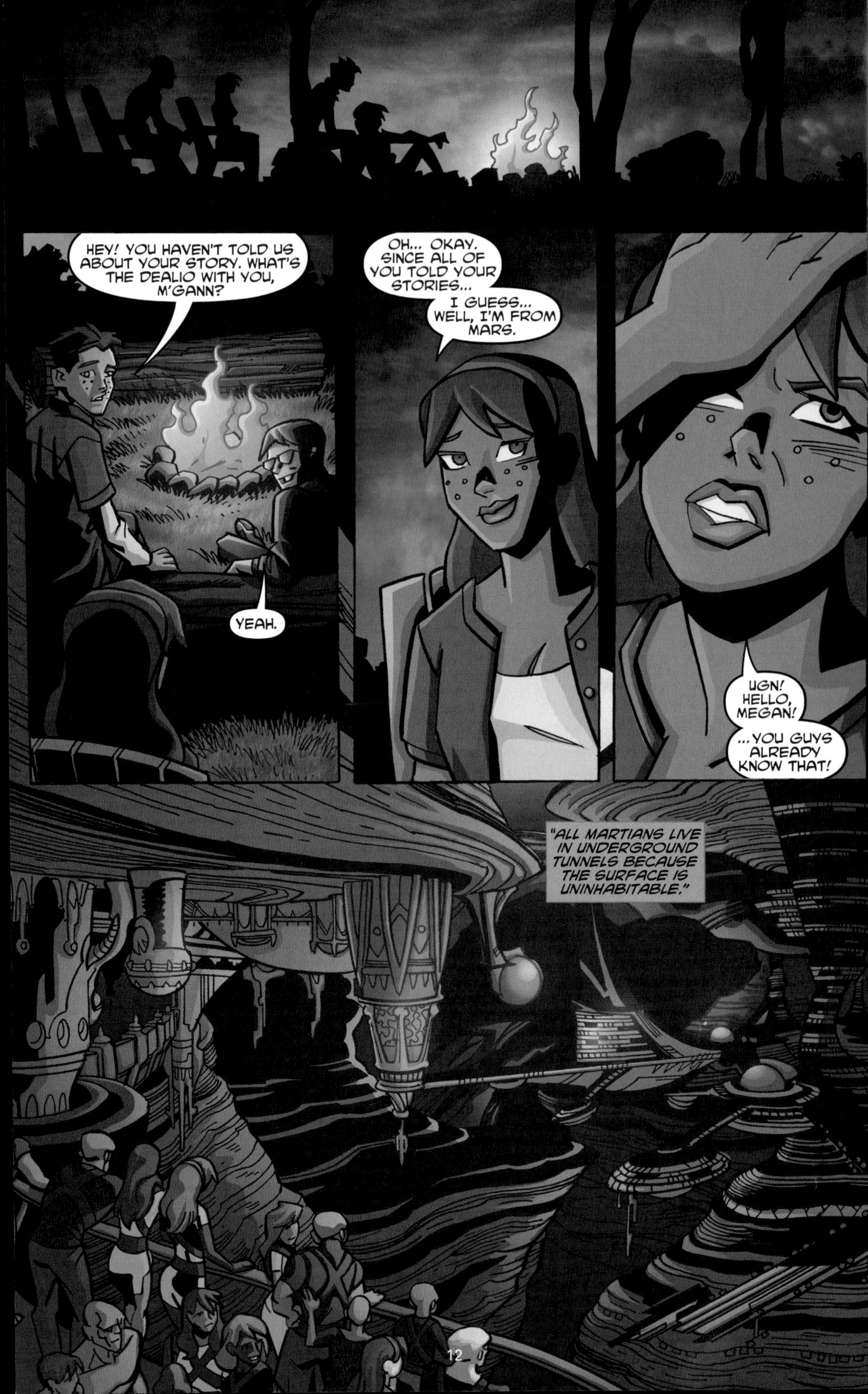

HEY! YOU HAVEN'T TOLD US ABOUT YOUR STORY. WHAT'S THE DEALIO WITH YOU, M'GANN?
YEAH.
OH... OKAY. SINCE ALL OF YOU TOLD YOUR STORIES...
I GUESS... WELL, I'M FROM MARS.
UGN! HELLO, MEGAN!
...YOU GUYS ALREADY KNOW THAT!
"ALL MARTIANS LIVE IN UNDERGROUND TUNNELS BECAUSE THE SURFACE IS UNINHABITABLE."

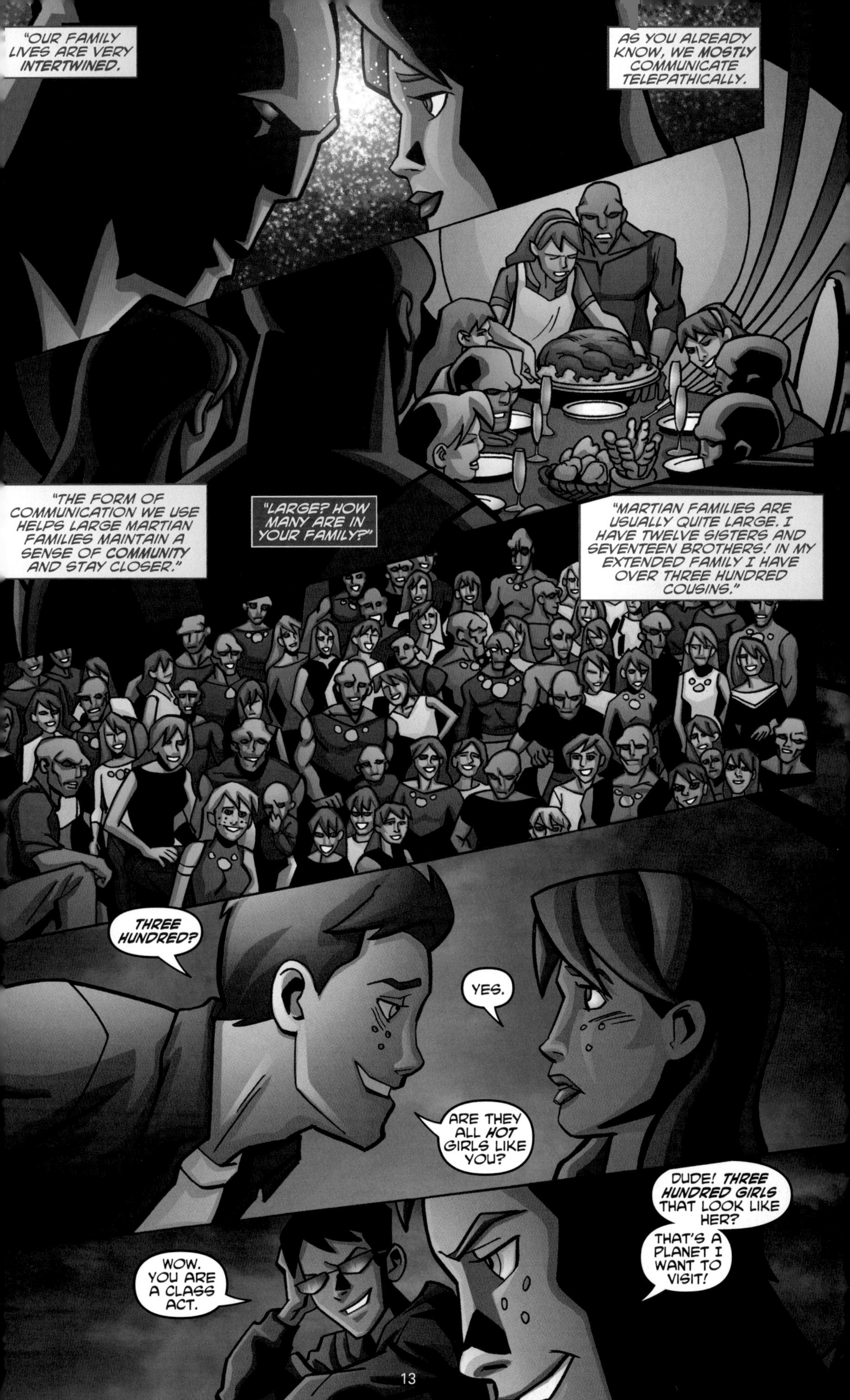
"OUR FAMILY LIVES ARE VERY INTERTWINED.
AS YOU ALREADY KNOW, WE MOSTLY COMMUNICATE TELEPATHICALLY.
"THE FORM OF COMMUNICATION WE USE HELPS LARGE MARTIAN FAMILIES MAINTAIN A SENSE OF COMMUNITY AND STAY CLOSER."
"LARGE? HOW MANY ARE IN YOUR FAMILY?"
"MARTIAN FAMILIES ARE USUALLY QUITE LARGE. I HAVE TWELVE SISTERS AND SEVENTEEN BROTHERS! IN MY EXTENDED FAMILY I HAVE OVER THREE HUNDRED COUSINS."
THREE HUNDRED?
YES.
ARE THEY ALL HOT GIRLS LIKE YOU?
DUDE! THREE HUNDRED GIRLS THAT LOOK LIKE HER?
THAT'S A PLANET I WANT TO VISIT!
WOW. YOU ARE A CLASS ACT.

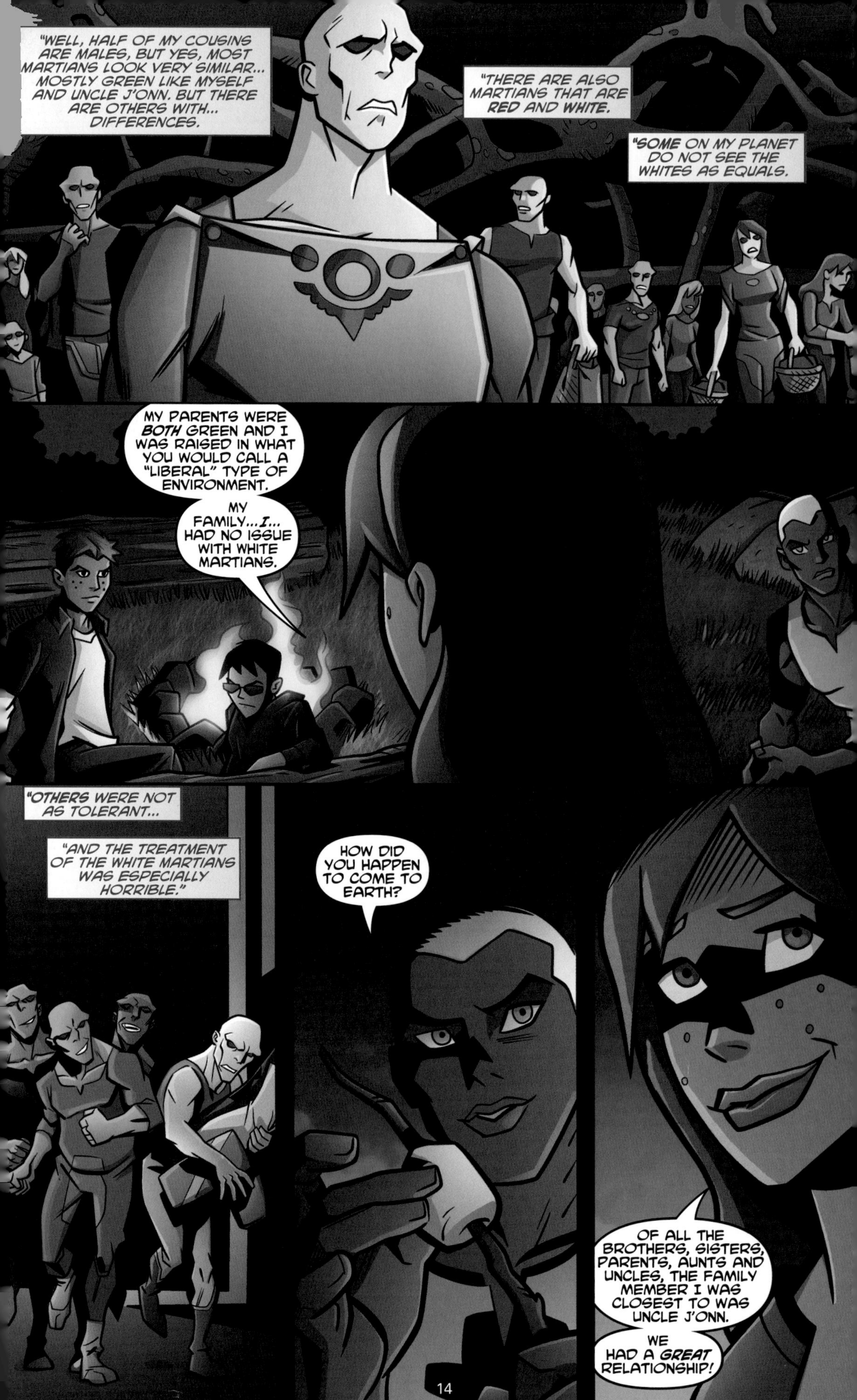
"WELL, HALF OF MY COUSINS ARE MALES, BUT YES, MOST MARTIANS LOOK VERY SIMILAR... MOSTLY GREEN LIKE MYSELF AND UNCLE J'ONN. BUT THERE ARE OTHERS WITH... DIFFERENCES.
"THERE ARE ALSO MARTIANS THAT ARE RED AND WHITE.
"SOME ON MY PLANET DO NOT SEE THE WHITES AS EQUALS.
MY PARENTS WERE BOTH GREEN AND I WAS RAISED IN WHAT YOU WOULD CALL A "LIBERAL" TYPE OF ENVIRONMENT.
MY FAMILY... I... HAD NO ISSUE WITH WHITE MARTIANS.
"OTHERS WERE NOT AS TOLERANT...
"AND THE TREATMENT OF THE WHITE MARTIANS WAS ESPECIALLY HORRIBLE."
HOW DID YOU HAPPEN TO COME TO EARTH?
OF ALL THE BROTHERS, SISTERS, PARENTS, AUNTS AND UNCLES, THE FAMILY MEMBER I WAS CLOSEST TO WAS UNCLE J'ONN.
WE HAD A GREAT RELATIONSHIP!

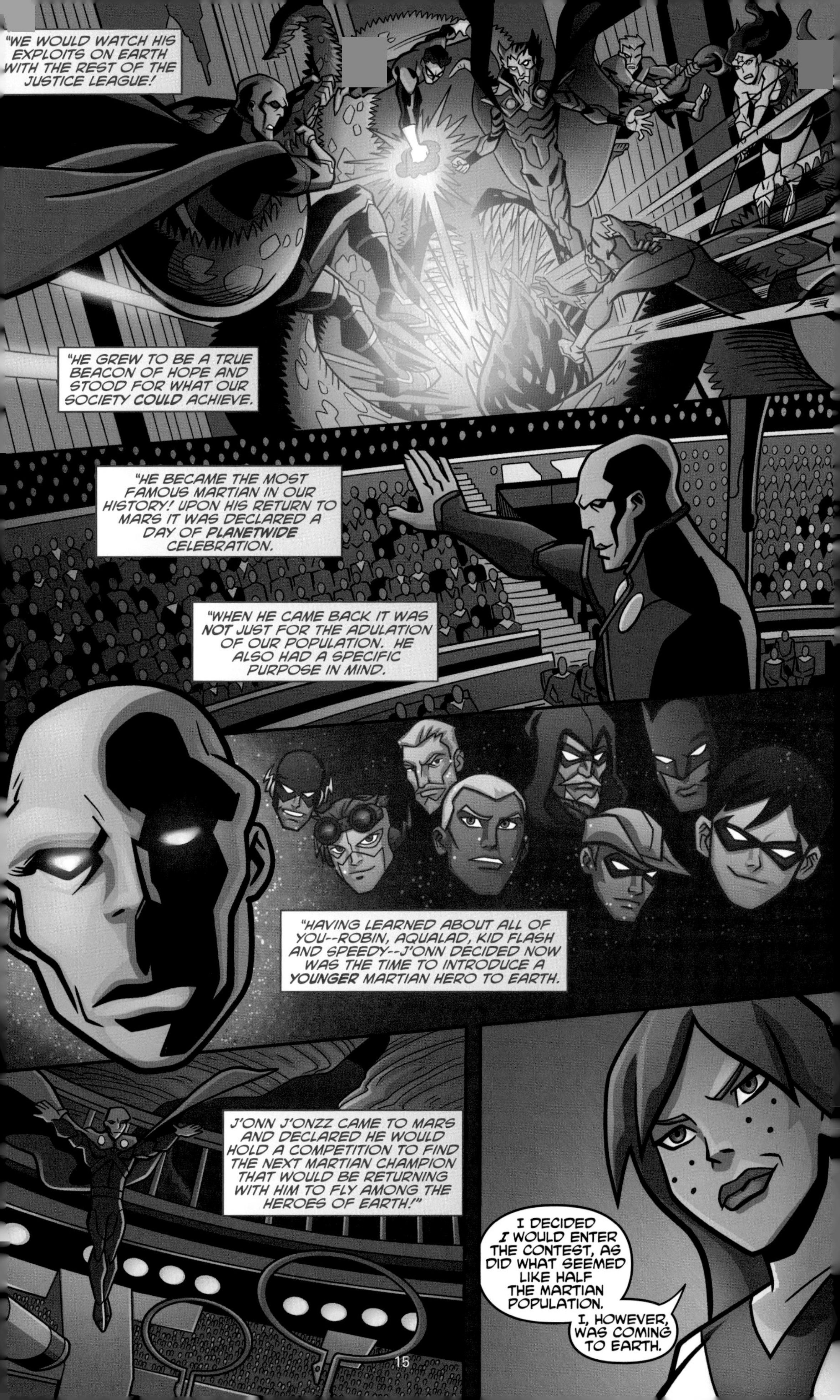

"WE WOULD WATCH HIS EXPLOITS ON EARTH WITH THE REST OF THE JUSTICE LEAGUE!
"HE GREW TO BE A TRUE BEACON OF HOPE AND STOOD FOR WHAT OUR SOCIETY COULD ACHIEVE.
"HE BECAME THE MOST FAMOUS MARTIAN IN OUR HISTORY! UPON HIS RETURN TO MARS IT WAS DECLARED A DAY OF PLANETWIDE CELEBRATION.
"WHEN HE CAME BACK IT WAS NOT JUST FOR THE ADULATION OF OUR POPULATION. HE ALSO HAD A SPECIFIC PURPOSE IN MIND.
"HAVING LEARNED ABOUT ALL OF YOU--ROBIN, AQUALAD, KID FLASH AND SPEEDY--J'ONN DECIDED NOW WAS THE TIME TO INTRODUCE A YOUNGER MARTIAN HERO TO EARTH.
J'ONN J'ONZZ CAME TO MARS AND DECLARED HE WOULD HOLD A COMPETITION TO FIND THE NEXT MARTIAN CHAMPION THAT WOULD BE RETURNING WITH HIM TO FLY AMONG THE HEROES OF EARTH!"
I DECIDED I WOULD ENTER THE CONTEST, AS DID WHAT SEEMED LIKE HALF THE MARTIAN POPULATION.
I, HOWEVER, WAS COMING TO EARTH.

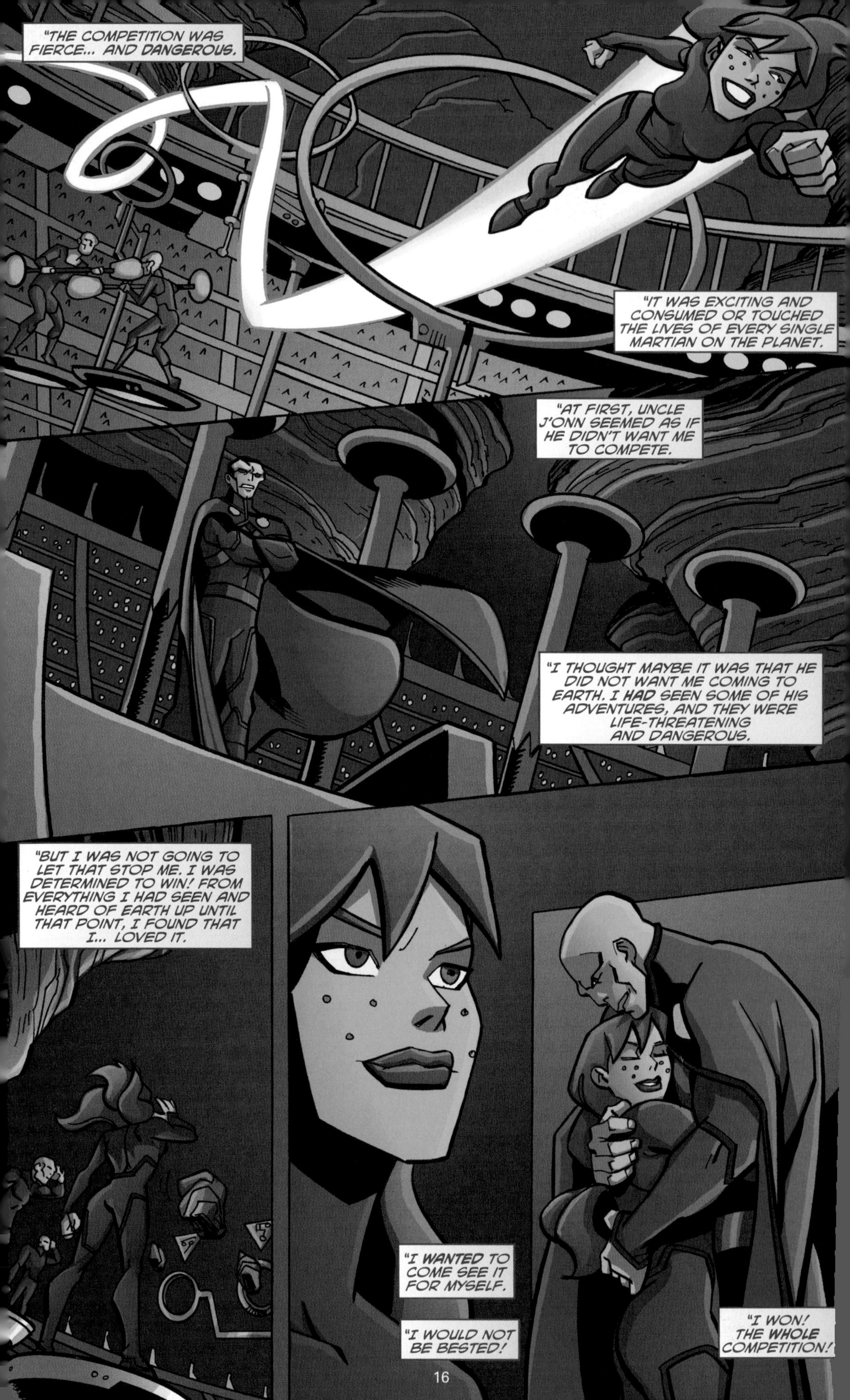
"THE COMPETITION WAS FIERCE... AND DANGEROUS.
"IT WAS EXCITING AND CONSUMED OR TOUCHED THE LIVES OF EVERY SINGLE MARTIAN ON THE PLANET.
"AT FIRST, UNCLE J'ONN SEEMED AS IF HE DIDN'T WANT ME TO COMPETE.
"I THOUGHT MAYBE IT WAS THAT HE DID NOT WANT ME COMING TO EARTH. I HAD SEEN SOME OF HIS ADVENTURES, AND THEY WERE LIFE-THREATENING AND DANGEROUS.
"BUT I WAS NOT GOING TO LET THAT STOP ME. I WAS DETERMINED TO WIN! FROM EVERYTHING I HAD SEEN AND HEARD OF EARTH UP UNTIL THAT POINT, I FOUND THAT I... LOVED IT.
"I WANTED TO COME SEE IT FOR MYSELF.
"I WOULD NOT BE BESTED!
"I WON! THE WHOLE COMPETITION!

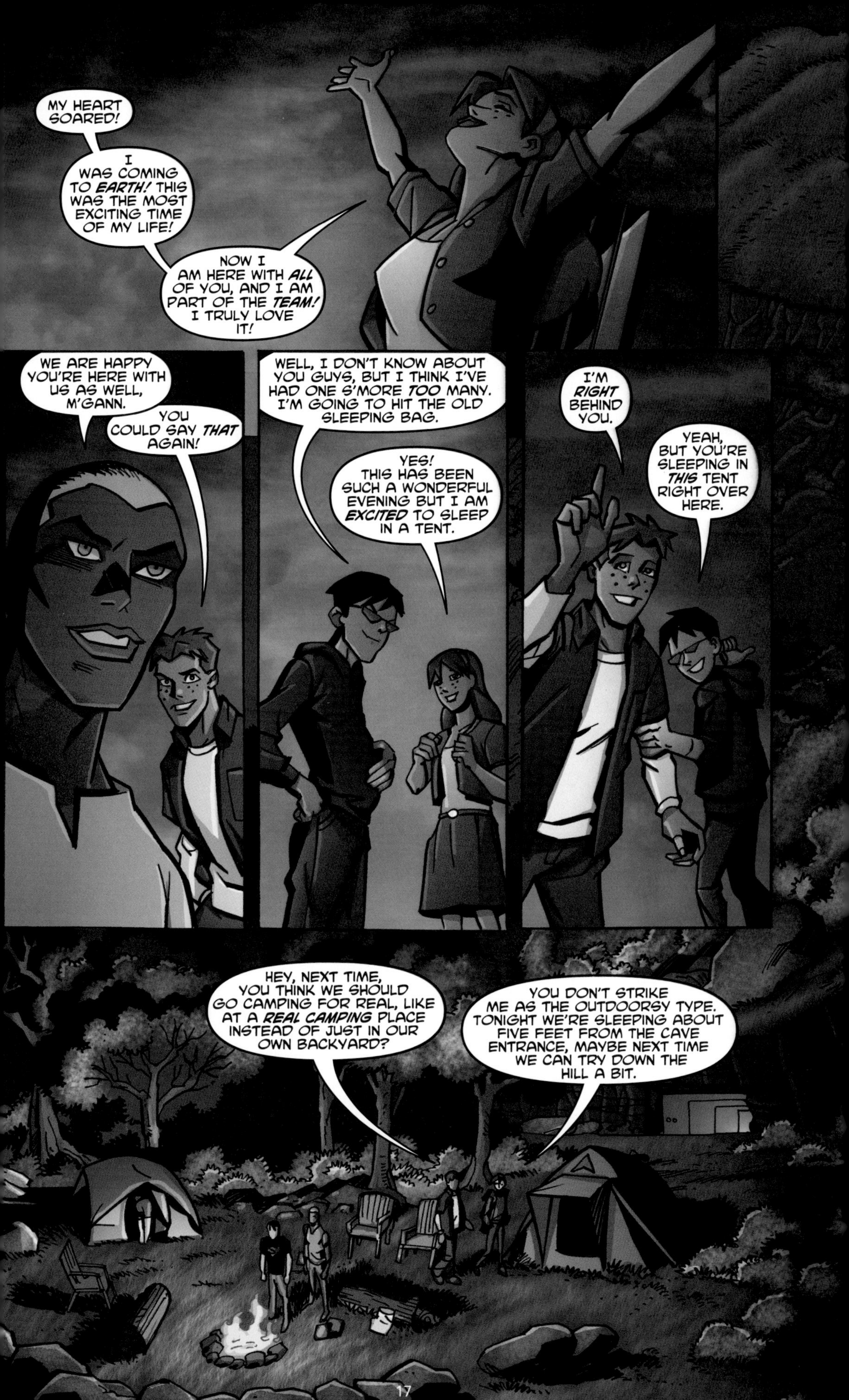

MY HEART SOARED!
I WAS COMING TO EARTH! THIS WAS THE MOST EXCITING TIME OF MY LIFE!
NOW I AM HERE WITH ALL OF YOU, AND I AM PART OF THE TEAM! I TRULY LOVE IT!
WE ARE HAPPY YOU'RE HERE WITH US AS WELL, M'GANN.
YOU COULD SAY THAT AGAIN!
WELL, I DON'T KNOW ABOUT YOU GUYS, BUT I THINK I'VE HAD ONE S'MORE TOO MANY. I'M GOING TO HIT THE OLD SLEEPING BAG.
YES! THIS HAS BEEN SUCH A WONDERFUL EVENING BUT I AM EXCITED TO SLEEP IN A TENT.
I'M RIGHT BEHIND YOU.
YEAH, BUT YOU'RE SLEEPING IN THIS TENT RIGHT OVER HERE.
HEY, NEXT TIME, YOU THINK WE SHOULD GO CAMPING FOR REAL, LIKE AT A REAL CAMPING PLACE INSTEAD OF JUST IN OUR OWN BACKYARD?
YOU DON'T STRIKE ME AS THE OUTDOORSY TYPE. TONIGHT WE'RE SLEEPING ABOUT FIVE FEET FROM THE CAVE ENTRANCE, MAYBE NEXT TIME WE CAN TRY DOWN THE HILL A BIT.

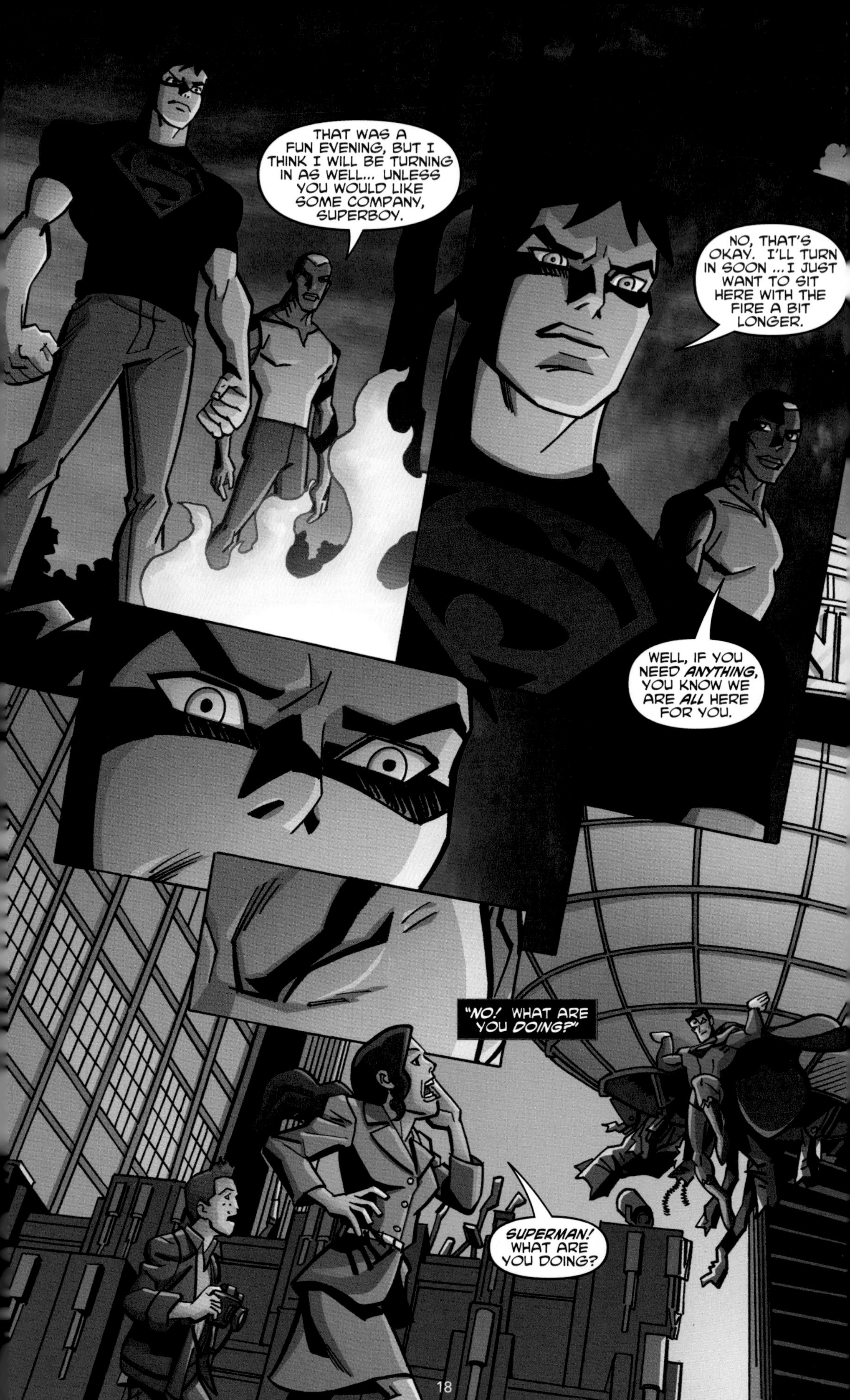
THAT WAS A FUN EVENING, BUT I THINK I WILL BE TURNING IN AS WELL... UNLESS YOU WOULD LIKE SOME COMPANY, SUPERBOY.
NO, THAT'S OKAY. I'LL TURN IN SOON ...I JUST WANT TO SIT HERE WITH THE FIRE A BIT LONGER.
WELL, IF YOU NEED *ANYTHING*, YOU KNOW WE ARE *ALL* HERE FOR YOU.
"*NO!* WHAT ARE YOU *DOING?*"
SUPERMAN! WHAT ARE YOU DOING?

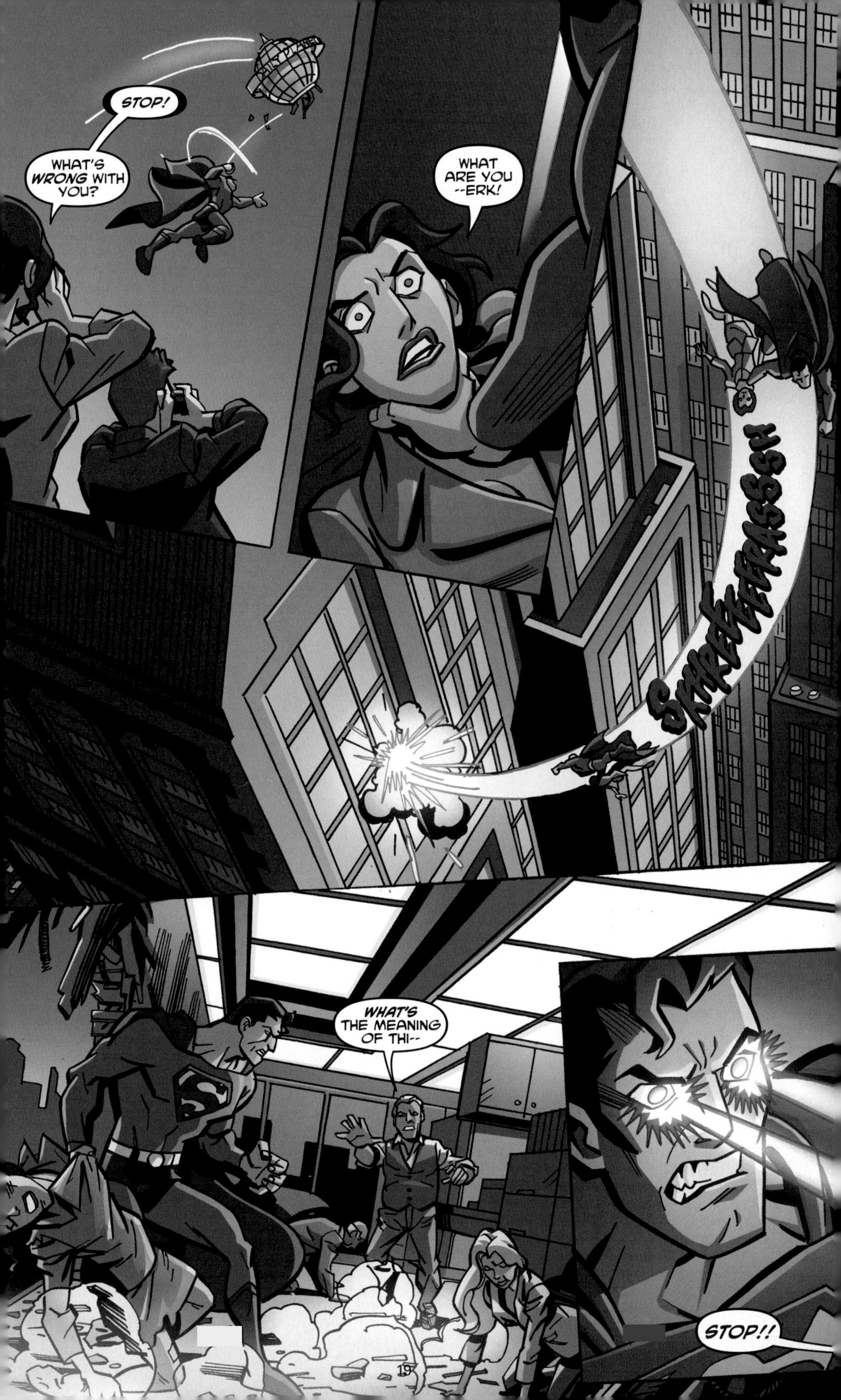

STOP!
WHAT'S *WRONG* WITH YOU?
WHAT ARE YOU --ERK!
SKREEEERASSSH
WHAT'S THE MEANING OF THI--
STOP!!

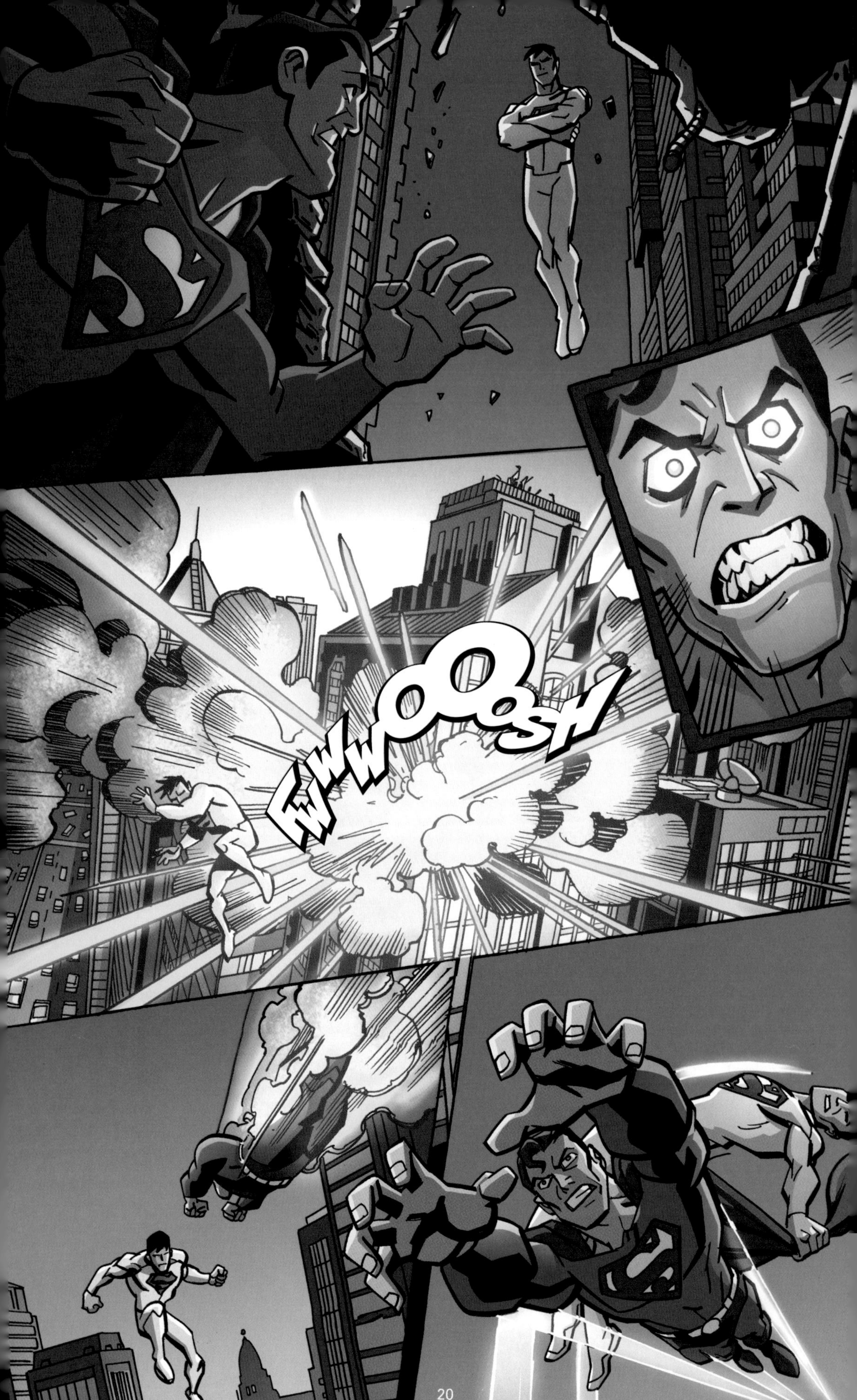
FWWWOOOSH

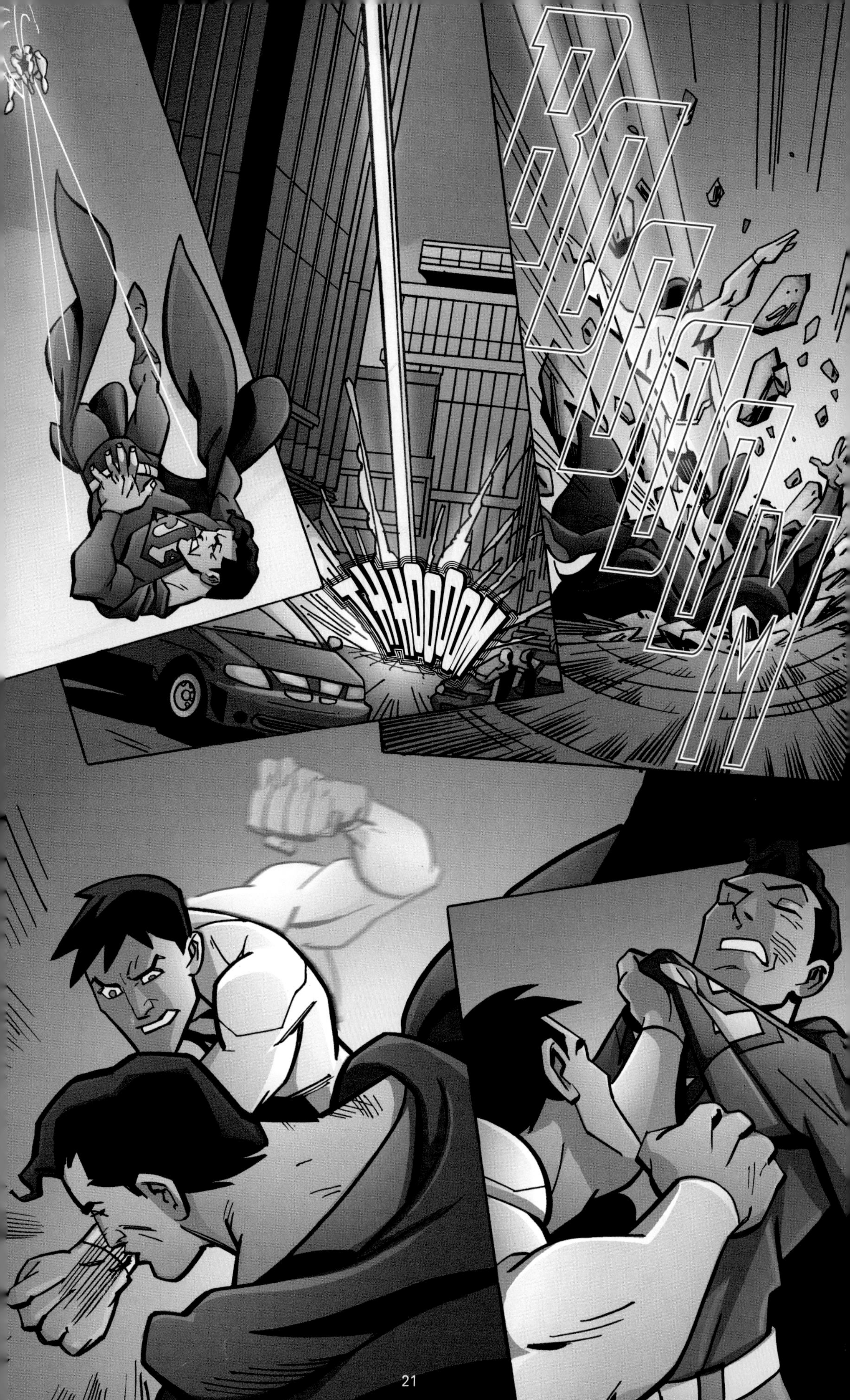
THOOOOM
BOOOOM

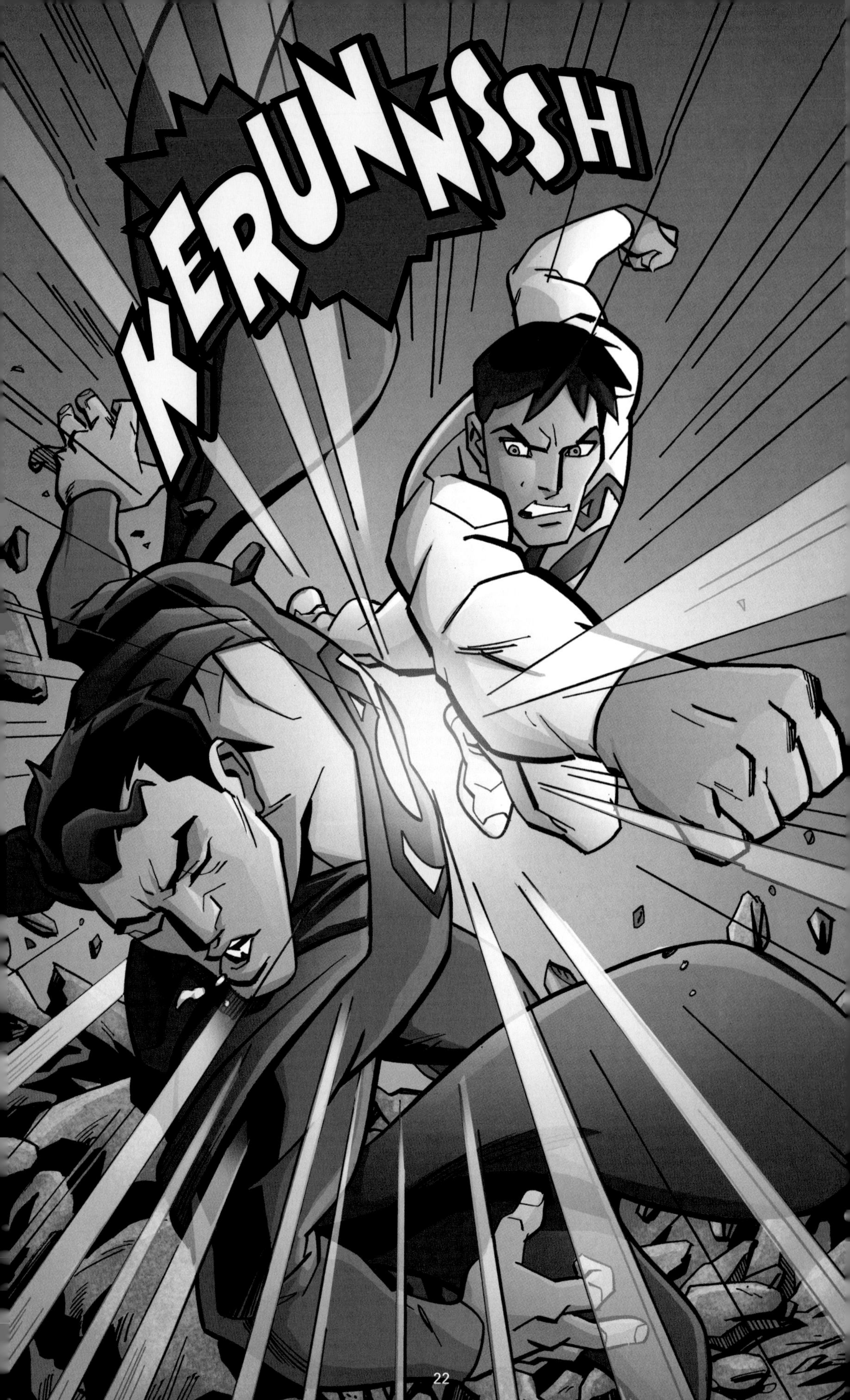
KERUNNSSH

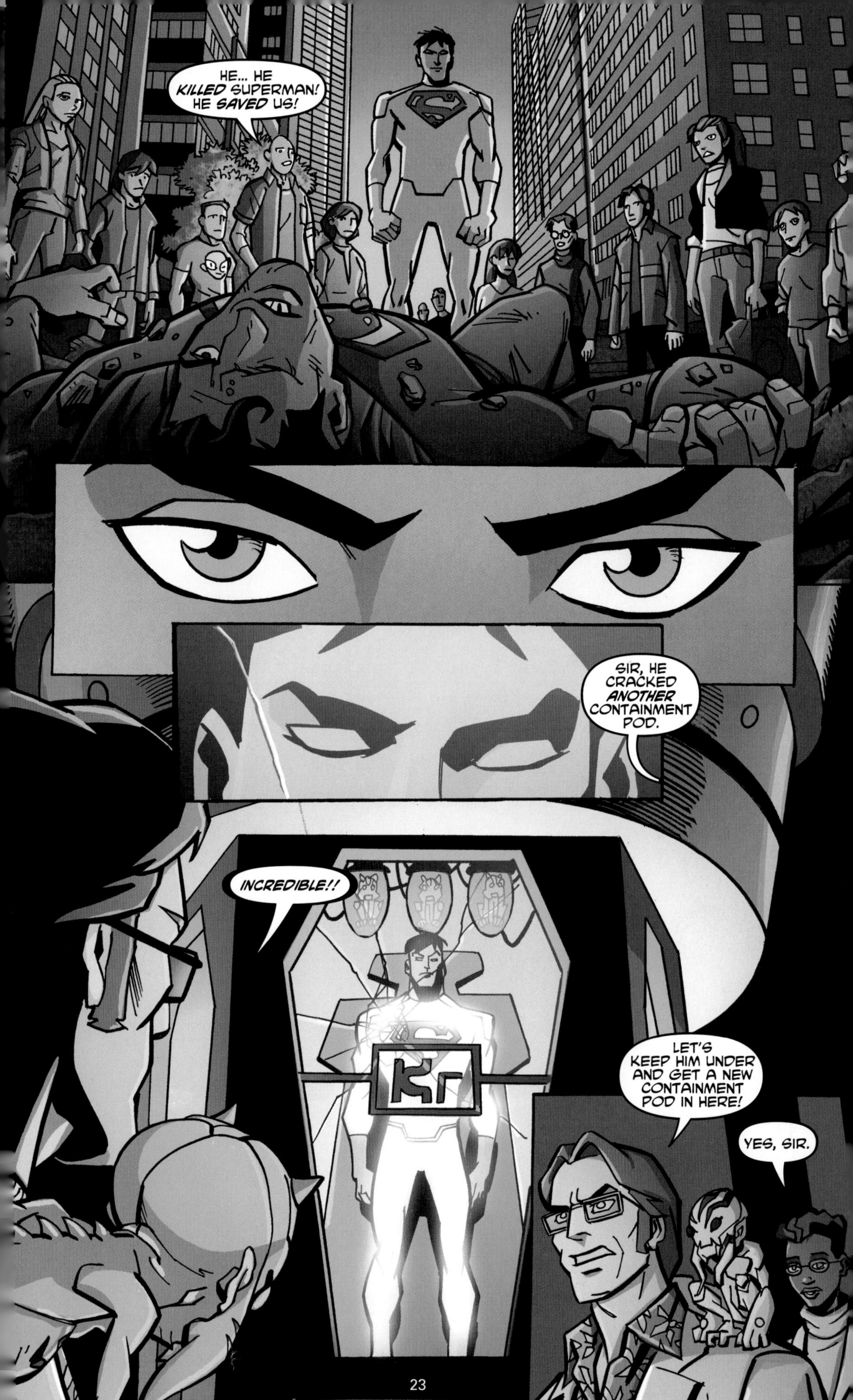

HE... HE KILLED SUPERMAN! HE SAVED US!
SIR, HE CRACKED ANOTHER CONTAINMENT POD.
INCREDIBLE!!
LET'S KEEP HIM UNDER AND GET A NEW CONTAINMENT POD IN HERE!
YES, SIR.

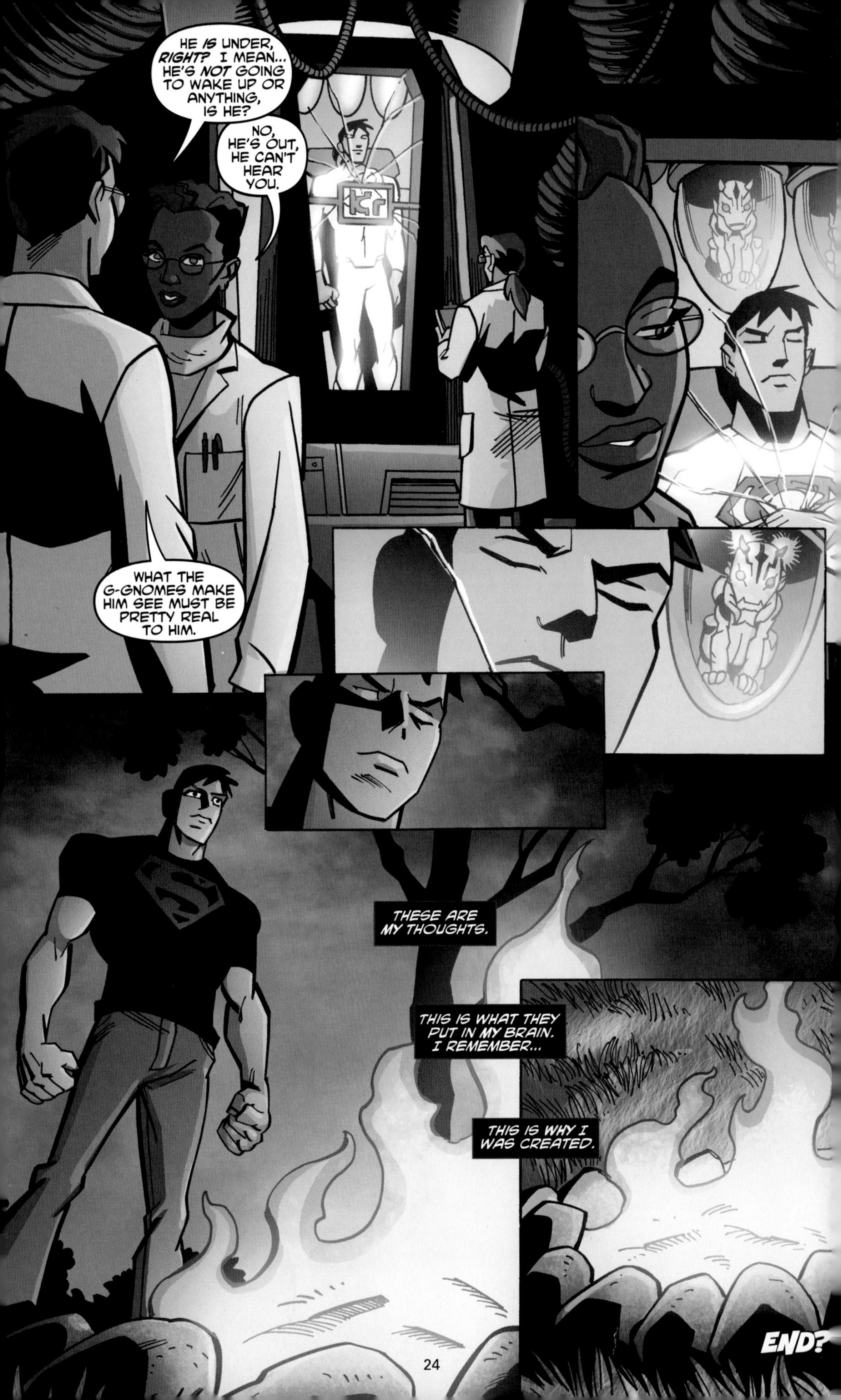
HE IS UNDER, RIGHT? I MEAN... HE'S NOT GOING TO WAKE UP OR ANYTHING, IS HE?
NO, HE'S OUT, HE CAN'T HEAR YOU.
WHAT THE G-GNOMES MAKE HIM SEE MUST BE PRETTY REAL TO HIM.
THESE ARE MY THOUGHTS.
THIS IS WHAT THEY PUT IN MY BRAIN. I REMEMBER...
THIS IS WHY I WAS CREATED.
END?

CAN YOUNG JUSTICE TURN THINGS AROUND...?

Read the next action-packed
adventure to find out!

only from...

 STONE ARCH BOOKS™
a capstone imprint   www.capstonepub.com

ART BALTAZAR WRITER

Art Baltazar is a cartoonist machine from the heart of Chicago! He defines cartoons and comics not only as an art style, but as a way of life. Currently, Art is the creative force behind *The New York Times* best-selling, Eisner Award-winning, DC Comics series Tiny Titans, and the co-writer for Billy Batson and the Magic of SHAZAM! and co-creator of Superman Family Adventures. Art is living the dream! He draws comics and never has to leave the house. He lives with his lovely wife, Rose, big boy Sonny, little boy Gordon, and little girl Audrey. Right on!

FRANCO AURELIANI WRITER

Bronx, New York born writer and artist Franco Aureliani has been drawing comics since he could hold a crayon. Currently residing in upstate New York with his wife, Ivette, and son, Nicolas, Franco spends most of his days in a Batcave-like studio where he produces DC's Tiny Titans comics. In 1995, Franco founded Blindwolf Studios, an independent art studio where he and fellow creators can create children's comics. Franco is the creator, artist, and writer of Weirdsville, L'il Creeps, and Eagle All Star, as well as the co-creator and writer of Patrick the Wolf Boy. When he's not writing and drawing, Franco also teaches high school art.

CHRISTOPHER JONES ARTIST

Christopher Jones is a professional illustrator and comic book artist. He has worked on Young Justice, The Batman Strikes!, and many other books for DC Comics.

GLOSSARY

beacon (BEE-kuhn)--a light or fire used as a signal or warning, or a shining example of something

exploits (EK-sploits)--brave or daring deeds

extort (ek-STORT)--to obtain by blackmail, force, or illegal power

intentions (in-TEN-shuhns)--things that you mean to do

intertwined (in-tur-TWINED)--inseparably connected, or united by winding something around something else

paralyzed (PAIR-uh-lized)--a loss of the power to move the body or its parts, or helpless or unable to function

ringmaster (RING-mass-tur)--the person in charge of performances at a circus

telepathically (tel-uh-PATH-ik-lee)--communicating directly from one mind to another

trauma (TRAW-muh)--a severe physical injury, or emotional shock

uninhabitable (un-in-HAB-it-uh-buhl)--unable to be lived in

VISUAL QUESTIONS & PROMPTS

1. At the end of this comic book, do you think Superboy is in the containment pod, or actually there at the camp site? Why?

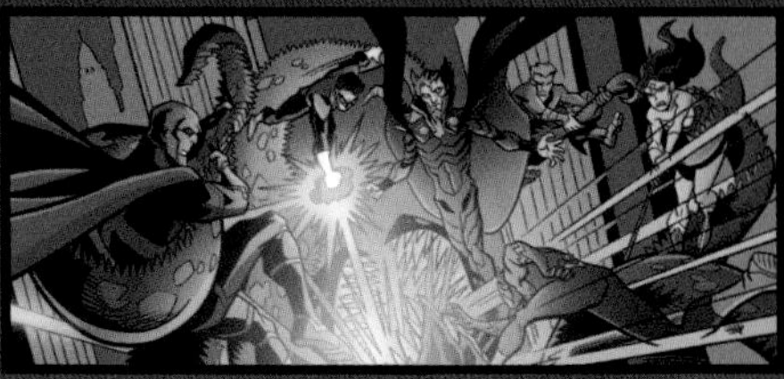

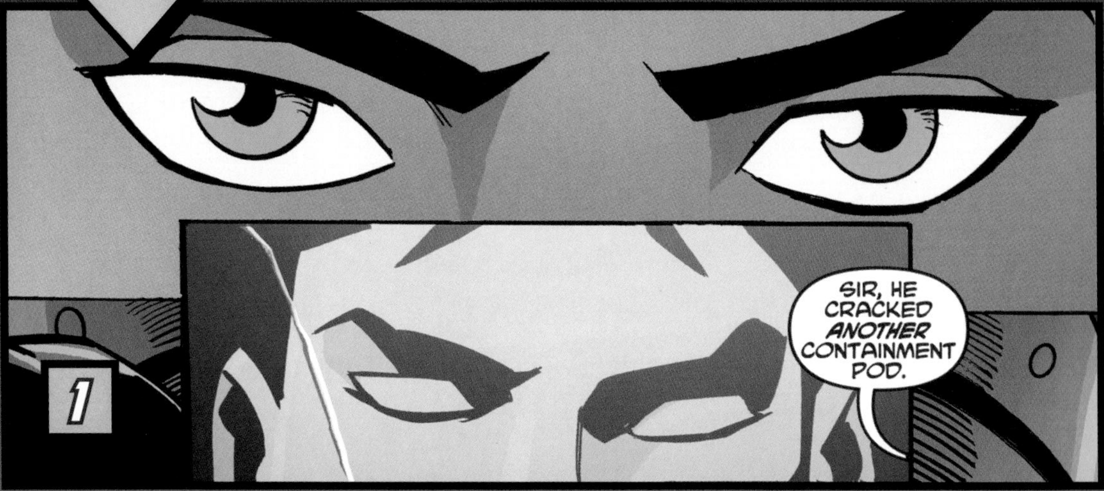
1
SIR, HE CRACKED ANOTHER CONTAINMENT POD.

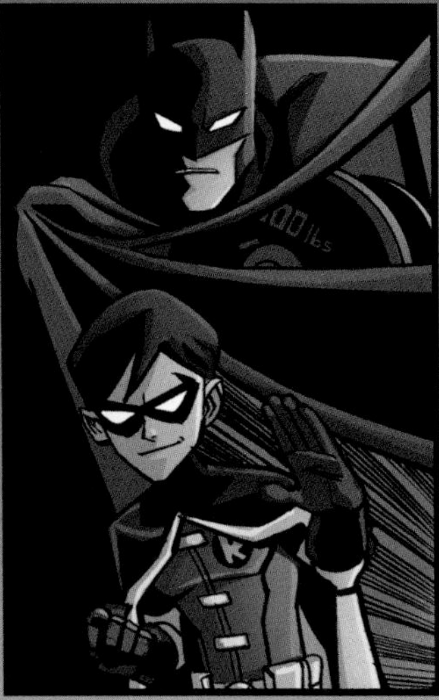

2. The title of this book is "Fears." Identify fears that Megan, Superboy, and Robin have in this story.

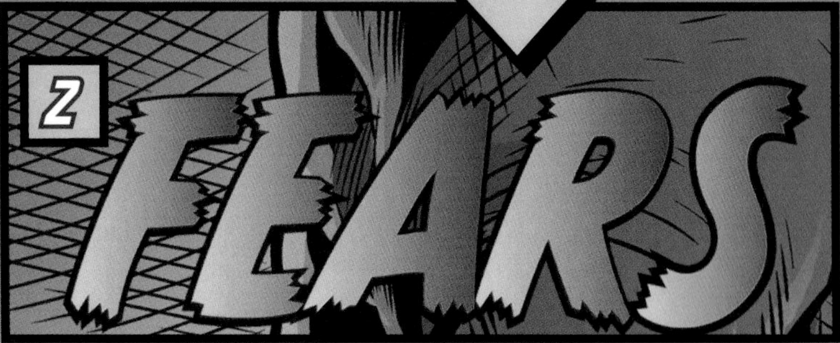
2
FEARS

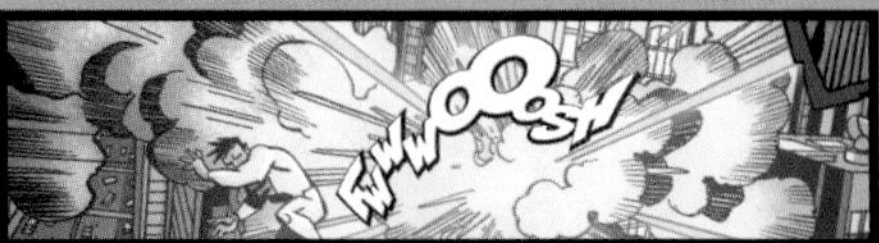
WWWOOOSH

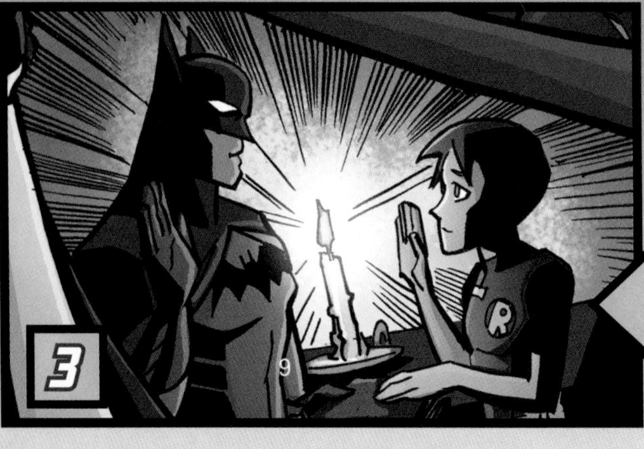
3

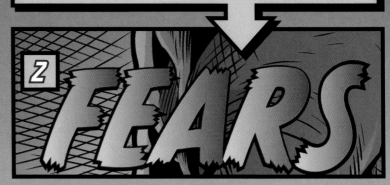

3. What do you think is happening in this panel? Read the surrounding panels on page 9 for clues.

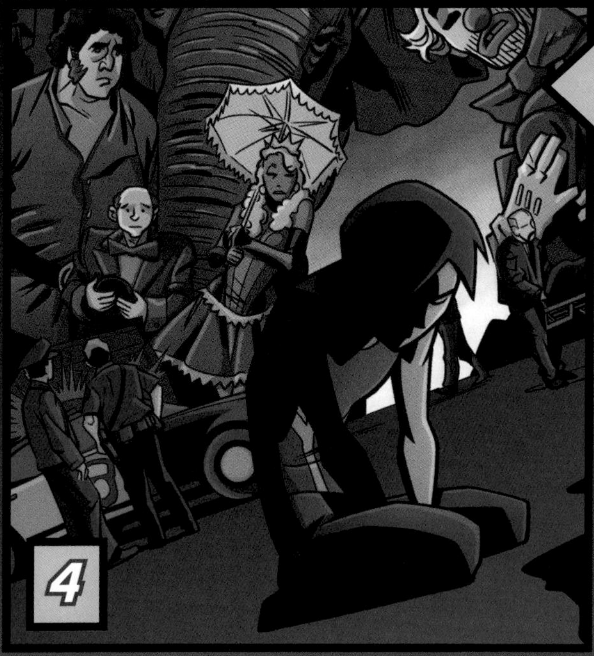
4

4. Why do you think Batman doesn't want Robin to tell others about his origin story?

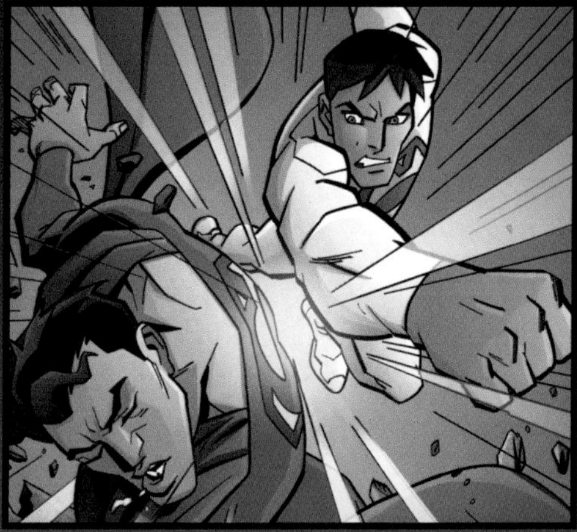

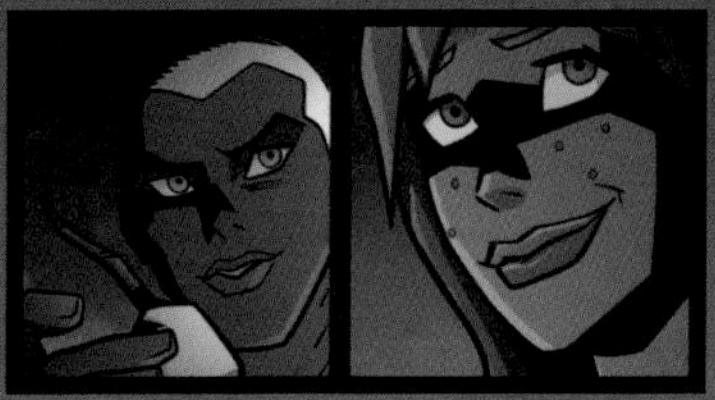

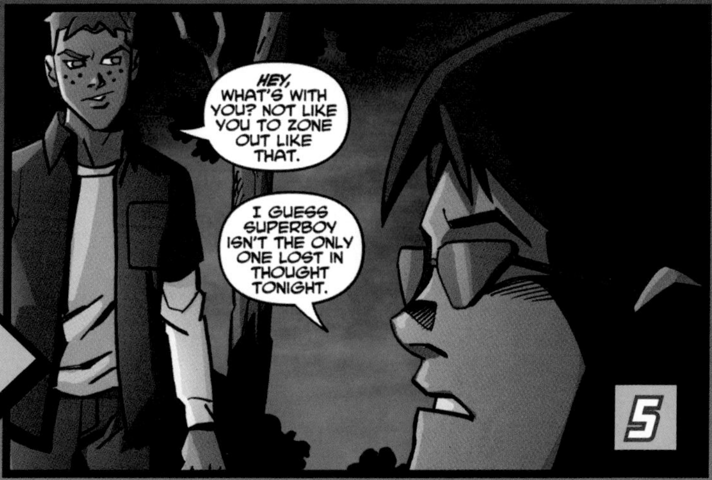
HEY, WHAT'S WITH YOU? NOT LIKE YOU TO ZONE OUT LIKE THAT.
I GUESS SUPERBOY ISN'T THE ONLY ONE LOST IN THOUGHT TONIGHT.
5

5. What was Robin thinking about when he zoned out? How do you know?

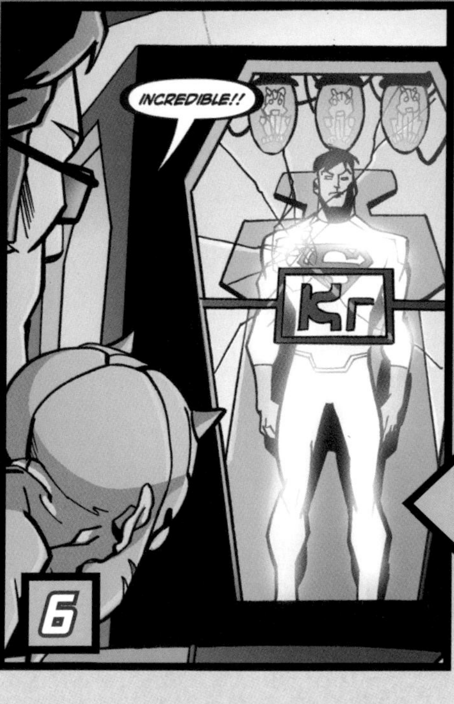
INCREDIBLE!!
Kr
6

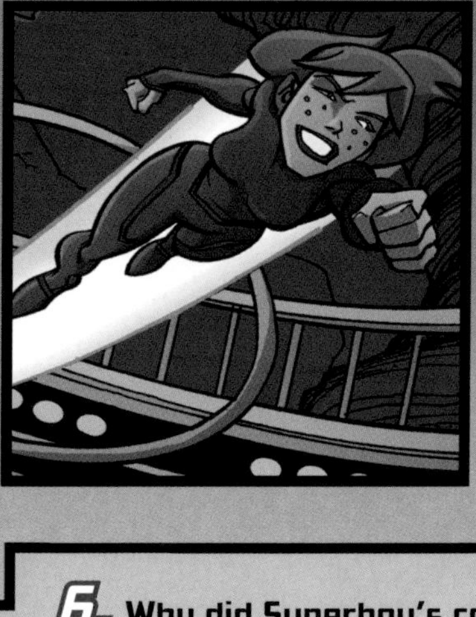

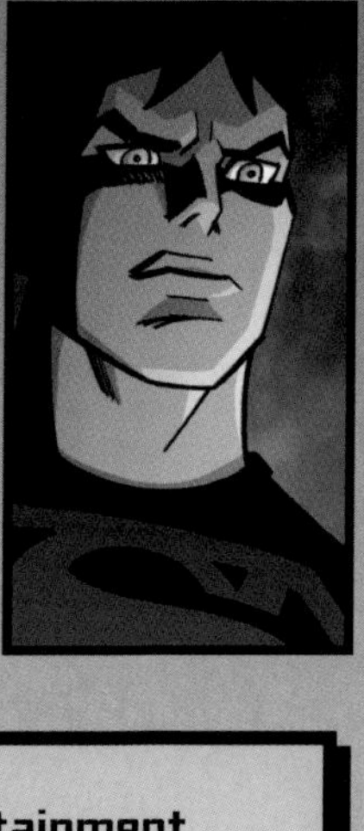

6. Why did Superboy's containment pod get cracked? Re-read the part of this book where Superboy remembers his time spent in the containment pod.

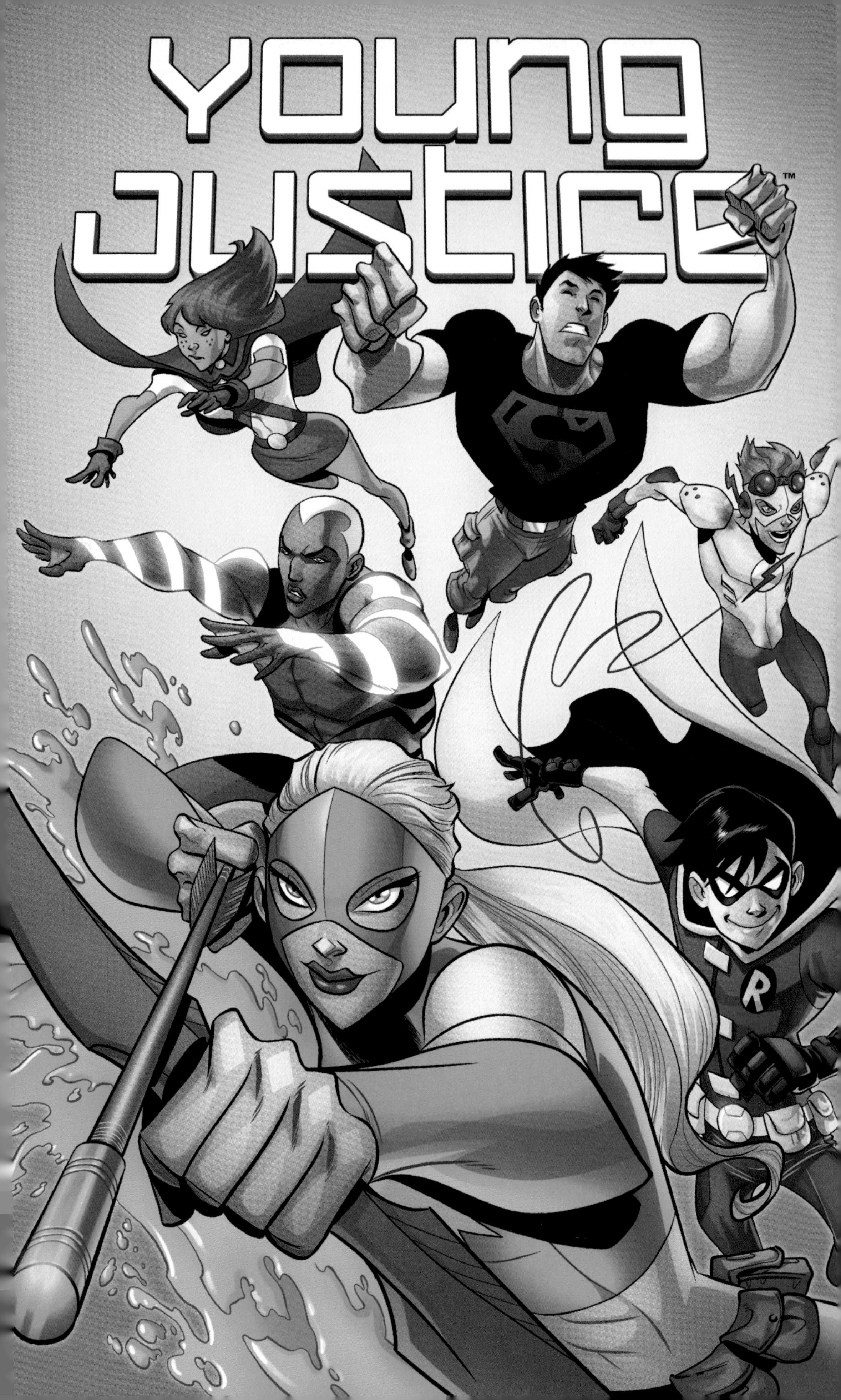
YOUNG JUSTICE™

READ THEM ALL!

HAUNTED

MONKEY BUSINESS

HACK AND YOU SHALL FIND

BY HOOK OR BY WEB

CAMPFIRE SECRETS

FEARS

RABBIT HOLES

WONDERLAND

young
Justice™